# HOG-TIED HERO

Maintaining order in a cow town, veteran Marshal Aaron McLean takes on more than he bargains for. Lyle Cameron is the most ruthless, the most powerful rancher in the territory. His feckless son is guilty of murdering the local undertaker. Marshal McLean knows that it is his duty to bring the killer in, but this will mean challenging the formidable Lyle Cameron. To make matters worse, the local community is stirred into civil strife over scandalous events at the saloon, Porky's Pride.

MARK BANNERMAN

# HOG-TIED HERO

*Complete and Unabridged*

LINFORD
*Leicester*

First published in Great Britain in 2004

First Linford Edition
published 2005

British Library CIP Data

Bannerman, Mark
    Hog-tied hero.—Large print ed.—
Linford western library
1. Western stories
2. Large type books
I. Title
823.9'14 [F]

ISBN 1–84395–585–7

Published by
F. A. Thorpe (Publishing)
Anstey, Leicestershire

Set by Words & Graphics Ltd.
Anstey, Leicestershire
Printed and bound in Great Britain by
T. J. International Ltd., Padstow, Cornwall

This book is printed on acid-free paper

This book is dedicated to my canine friend

TIM

# 1

It was near midnight when the blast of gunfire roused Marshal Aaron McLean. With his feet on the desk in his office, he'd just dozed off, having pulled the brim of his hat over his eyes, but soon he realized where the shots had come from. Down the street, the inaugural opening of the new saloon *Porky's Pride* was in full swing, and with a whole bunch of Lyle Cameron's cowboys having ridden in to sample the drinks on the house, it sounded as if things were getting over riotous.

Aaron McLean was a sixty year old, bone-seasoned Texan, spoke in a slow drawl and sported a cookie-duster mustache. He had squint lines around his eyes like spiders' legs. He'd been the elected town marshal of Nelly's Nipple for a decade. He enjoyed his work, providing there was no trouble. He preferred the jail in his office to be empty. In fact he usually slept behind the bars himself, having no alternative accommodation. He was somewhat under six feet tall and scrawny lean. For the sake of his liver, the doctor had advised him to observe temperance. So he'd sworn off the hard stuff, sticking to lemon juice or milk, though the latter tended to leave a skim of cream on his mustache.

He debated whether or not he should venture down to calm the festivities. Previously, he'd figured it would be best to keep out the way and let the fun take its course, but with those cowboys firing off their six-shooters, albeit in the air, somebody might get hurt. Especially Lucy May and her soiled doves on the upper floor. Lucy May had done well to gather together all her local girls and set them up in *Porky's Pride* in time for the opening night. But if the bar room's ceilings weren't bullet proof, the girls' clients might be getting more excitement than they'd paid for.

For a moment his eyes hitched onto his set of false teeth reclining on the desk between the can he'd been spooning beans from, and his left boot. The teeth were leering at him. He hated them. What damned good were false teeth that you had to take out before you ate or even laughed? They robbed life of its spontaneity. And if you sneezed, you were likely to kill somebody. His lips just weren't strong enough to restrain them.

He picked them up and rammed them into his mouth. The fact was that for the first forty years of his life he'd never cleaned his teeth once, not even with a twig. It was only after his wife Hilda, now sadly departed, had insisted that he used one of those new-fangled toothbrushes, that his tusks had gone rotten. One day, he told himself, he'd track down that horseback dentist who'd charged him the earth for pulling them out and fitting the denture. He'd give him a piece of his mind; maybe he'd sneeze in his direction.

Standing up, he felt the familiar stiffness of rheumatism in his legs. He stamped it out. He strapped on his gun and hoped he wouldn't have need of it. He paused to glance at the tintype photograph of Hilda that occupied pride of place on his desk. He tenderly touched it with his callused thumb. He recalled her scornful snort at everything he ever did. She had been a most contrary woman, ugly as galvanized sin, forever going on about how she'd married below her station. She'd always fobbed him off, saying she couldn't stand kissing a man with stale gravy caked in his mustache.

He couldn't understand why he pined for her more each day. Sometimes, sitting at his desk, he felt downright lonely, like a preacher on pay night.

He left his office, crossed the boardwalk and stepped down onto the wide street. The saloon was on the opposite side, some fifty yards along. The street was so broad that freight wagons could turn around in one movement. It was criss-crossed with wide wheel furrows. Right now the night was as black as the inside of a cow's belly, and within seconds he was cursing as he stumbled ankle deep through a heap of horse apples, swearing that it was about time some method of street lighting was introduced. He'd suggest it at the next meeting of the town's council.

But down the street there was plenty of light, and plenty of noise. It emanated from the open windows and doors of *Porky's Pride*. The place was nigh bouncing with its internal activity, and as Aaron approached, passing various closed stores and clapboard houses, he stamped his boots clean. More shooting sparked off from the saloon, coming with the intensity of a Gatling gun, and with it, the wild hooting of cowboys, the tinkling of a piano and the voice of a female singer rendering *Oh Susanna!*

The marshal swallowed back his

apprehensions. The fact that he might be outnumbered by twenty-to-one troubled him, but he knew the town paid him to maintain law and order, and he didn't want Mayor Tresswell accusing him of shirking his duties. He wished he hadn't given his deputy, Gregg Mason, time off to visit his sick aunt at Fallow Springs.

He reached the saloon, pausing briefly to glance at the great painting of Porky the pig that adorned the outside wall adjacent to the batwings. Porky was the inspiration for the establishment's name — *Porky's Pride*. It was easy to see why the portrayal had caused consternation at the local townswomen's guild. Aaron grinned to himself before stepping over a sprawled drunkard snoring it off on the boardwalk and pushing through the batwings into the saloon's interior. He made his entrance as inconspicuous as possible, standing with his back to the wall, just inside.

The long room was packed to the rafters, lit by a multitude of oil lamps.

At one end of the bar, a fella had a rattlesnake in a jar, and was taking bets as to who could stare into the reptile's eyes and not flinch as it made its dart. A group of loud-mouthed cowpunchers fondled saucily clad hurdy-gurty gals, and the air was thick with both baccy and gun smoke, reeking with alcohol, sweat and perfume. The female singer, Violette La Plante, was on the raised platform, sounding as if she had lungs of leather as she competed with the racket of clinking glasses, garrulous voices and general mayhem. Her face was by no means the prettiest in the world, but it was her legs that attracted the eye. So high was the slit in the front of her skirt, that her rose-coloured garters were revealed in all their glory. Apart from bawdy-house girls, Aaron had never seen so far up the inside of a real, live woman's thighs, least of all Hilda's.

On the sober side of the great, bustling bar, the fine back-drop mirror had already been cracked by an errant bullet. Above the mirror hung the classic figure of a pale skinned, dark haired nude reclining on a couch, her curlies partially concealed by the rose she clutched. Her other arm lay across her left breast, but her slim white fingers cupped its partner, emphasising her cherry-pink nipple. There was no denying her beauty. At the bottom of the gilt frame, was a plate inscribed 'NELLY — QUEEN OF HEAVEN'S ANGELS.' She was the lady, long moved on, who had given rise to the name of the town in her titular way.

Aaron wondered what the reaction of the town's womenfolk would be if the picture of Nelly was displayed on the outside wall, instead of Porky's. But right now he had more important matters to consider. How was he going to calm the place down? There was far too much hardware on show and the ceiling was peppered with bullet holes. Some neighbouring settlements had banned the carrying of weapons in town, and maybe it was something he

8

would have to consider for the future, but the ban wouldn't be easy to enforce because Lyle Cameron's cowpunchers, all hoodlums, figured they were a law unto themselves. He knew some of their names — Brad Higgins, Seth Cranshaw who was one of a twin, Johnny James and a half dozen more, and of course Lyle Cameron's twenty-year-old son, Billy, who was a flannel-mouth and spoilt sick by his father. He'd been sent east for schooling but was expelled because his quick temper had got the better of him. He'd beaten up a teacher and had returned home to indulge his penchant for liquor, wild women and gambling at his pa's expense.

Aaron noticed the sign displayed at the foot of the staircase.

LUCY MAY'S PARLOR UPSTAIRS
SATISFACTION GUARANTEED,
OR MONEY REFUNDED
COWBOYS: PLEASE REMOVE
SPURS BEFORE BEING SERVICED

Aaron's eyes twinkled for a second, but then were drawn to the far end of the bar room. Billy Cameron was the dealer in a game of poker, along with a cowboy friend, and a group of local men which included the town's undertaker, the bespectacled Silas Fogwell who was so thin he resembled a snake on stilts. His bean-pole, black garbed body reminded Aaron of a crow pecking at the profit from other folk's misfortunes.

Billy Cameron was dealing with savage speed, flipping the cards in scattered piles. The players gathered up their cards, riffled through them and waited.

But right now a change had come over Silas Fogwell. His narrow face had started to twitch and his cheeks showed a redness. Suddenly he stood up, throwing his cards down upon the baize, sending his chair toppling behind him. Made even taller by his stovepipe hat, he loomed above the other gamblers as they sat clutching pasteboards close to their bellies, the green baize before them scattered with piles of dollar pieces, cards and bottles of rye.

Fogwell's words, along with an accusing finger, were aimed directly at Billy Cameron, cutting through the general burble of the establishment.

'*I don't like cheaters, Billy Cameron!*'

# 2

All the drunken babble died out, even the singer and piano dribbled into silence as all eyes swung to the poker table and the men around it.

Young Billy tilted his head back, his face florid, gazed up at the undertaker and in a breathy voice, husky with liquor, said, 'I don't think I heard you right, Mister.'

'I can't make it no clearer, Billy Cameron. I saw you dealin' from the bottom of the pack. You're a damned cheat and maybe your pa should know about it.'

Billy's pug-face twitched with anger and this stimulated movement as men distanced themselves from the poker table, knocking over chairs as they hastily stepped back and crowded to the side to avoid the gunfire that generally followed such accusations.

Cheating was a serious matter, like horse theft.

One of the other card players lifted his arm to restrain the undertaker and cried out, 'Silas, hold your tongue. You've had too much snake water!'

Angrily, Fogwell brushed him aside. 'Pull in your horns, Kid,' he snarled. 'You don't scare me!'

Billy stood up. 'Nobody calls me a cheat and gets away with it,' he hissed, his eyes wild; he brushed back his coat to reveal the big, walnut-butted Colt .45 in a flashy holster at his hip. Around the room, some of his cowboy friends yelled out encouragement.

Murder, fuelled by alcohol, was in the air. Aaron knew he had to act.

'Hold hard, you two,' he yelled. 'Calm down!'

For a second, Fogwell seemed taken aback, his eyes hidden behind the opaqueness of his tinted spectacles. Aaron rushed forward, his intention to place himself between the two adversaries, but suddenly Fogwell did a foolish thing. He put his hand into the pocket of his frock coat.

Aaron was no more than a yard from them when the gun appeared in Billy's hand and its roar erupted. Into its reverberation, women were screaming and men shouting — and the undertaker was thrown backwards to land on the sawdust floor, his shirt-front a gory mess.

The marshal lowered himself to his knees, gazed at the fallen man. He'd seen death enough times to know that he was beyond recall. Then, slowly he lifted his gaze to meet the wide eyes of Billy Cameron. The boy was standing alone at the table, gunsmoke hanging to him like a shroud of guilt. He seemed in a sort of trance. He still held the big .45, but now it was pointed at Aaron. All around, the confusion of voices and movement had stilled; some folks stood with their mouths agape.

Calmly, Aaron said, 'You just drop the gun, Billy. I need to take you in.'

'Marshal,' cowpoke Seth Cranshaw

called out in slurred tones, 'Billy ain't done nothin' 'ceptin' defend hisself. Fogwell was goin' for his gun.'

Aaron didn't reply. Instead, he took hold of the undertaker's wrist and dragged his lifeless hand from the frock-coat pocket into which it had been plunged. Aaron reached into the pocket, felt around, pulled out all he found — a large polka-dot handkerchief. As he stood up, a great exhalation of breath cut through the surrounding throng.

'Drop the gun, Billy,' he repeated.

Billy drew his lips back in a grimace. Aaron noticed he was buck-toothed, like a rabbit. He'd sobered up with remarkable speed. He flexed his fingers, then released his hold on the gun, allowed it to drop into the sawdust.

'It was self defence, Marshal,' he gasped. 'I figured he was drawin' a gun.'

'Maybe classed as self defence,' Aaron drawled, 'maybe not. That'll be for the judge to decide. Meanwhile, I have to lock you up.'

15

'You can't lock him up, marshal,' somebody called out. 'He's Lyle Cameron's son!'

'Don't make no difference if he's the good Lord hisself,' Aaron commented. 'I'm arrestin' him for killin' Silas Fogwell.'

Standing at the end of the bar, Seth Cranshaw emitted a snarl. The fiery thread of fierce liquor was burning his guts. He reached for the half full rye bottle alongside him. 'Marshal,' he shouted, 'I said Billy was defendin' hisself. You ain't takin' him in.'

Aaron was turning to face Cranshaw when the hard-flung bottle struck his head. He staggered like a drunkard, then his legs buckled and he collapsed.

Despite being only semi-conscious, he was aware of boots thumping the floor around him, aware of the general exodus that was taking place. After that, he must have blacked out for a while.

In the confusion the big jar at the end of the bar had been knocked over.

16

Liberated, the rattlesnake it had contained side-wound across the bar-top and dropped down behind into the shadows between some beer kegs. Nobody noticed, not even the snake-owner who was too busy vacating the premises with his winnings.

When sensibility returned, Aaron raised himself slightly. He saw how blood was soaking in to the sawdust in front of his nose — his blood. His head felt as heavy as a cannon ball, or maybe an overfull water bladder that was about to burst. He drew out his handkerchief and staunched the blood.

A ring-encrusted hand touched his shoulder. It belonged to Bent Nose Beecher, the proprietor of the saloon, unmistakable with his crooked smeller and in his patterned-silk waistcoat and dandy shirt.

'Have a swig of this coffin varnish,' he said. 'It'll make you feel better.'

'Nope,' Aaron grunted. 'I've sworn off the hard stuff. Ain't lettin' that no-good Billy Cameron force me to break my word.' He felt around on the floor. 'Where's my teeth?' he enquired.

''Ere, Marshal,' Miss La Plante, the singer, announced, brushing aside the rather bedraggled feather that adorned her hair. 'When ze bottle hit you, ze teeth shot out. Went straight into a spittoon.'

'Holy smoke!' Aaron commented.

'Don't worry, *mon chéri*,' she said soothingly. 'I fished zem out for you.'

Aaron grunted his thanks, took the dentures and rammed them into his mouth.

He was helped to his unsteady feet, would've fallen had not Bent Nose Beecher and Violette La Plante supported his arms. He moved to the bar, leaned against it for support.

His eyes focussed on the lifeless body of Silas Fogwell.

Following his gaze, Bent Nose Beecher said, 'His undertakin' skills are sure gonna be missed. His apprentice is still green behind the ears. What a doggone lousy thing to happen on our

18

first night open. All we wanted was for folks to have some fun and get to like the place. Guess a touch of notoriety won't do us no harm though.'

The saloon proprietor stooped down and picked something up — Fogwell's spectacles which had fallen to the floor, miraculously unbroken. 'You better have these, Marshal,' he said.

'What for?' Aaron queried.

'Could be some sort of evidence. You never know.'

Aaron pulled a doubtful face, but he took them.

He was deeply troubled. Murder had been done — and he knew that it was his duty to go after the killer and arrest him, together with his bunky who had obstructed justice by throwing that bottle. And to make certain the law was enforced he would have to challenge the most powerful man in the territory — Billy's pa, Lyle Cameron.

# 3

Gregg Mason arrived back from his visit to Fallow Springs on the noon Concord stage, dismounting in Main Street. He was aware that his city suit was sweat-stained and creased by the hot, dusty journey. This had irked him, for he had caught the eye of the bosomy girl sitting opposite him more than once and he knew he was not looking his best. Unfortunately the girl, appearing remarkably cool, had remained on the coach as it continued onward and he had not even had the chance to ask her name. Twenty-year-old Gregg was tall and lean. He knew that he was a handsome hunk, and he was frequently looking in the mirror to make sure his sandy hair and boxcar mustache were in order; also to generally admire himself. He attracted girls like cats to catnip; he just couldn't help it. He was deputy marshal of Nelly's Nipple and soon he hoped to take over from Aaron McLean in the number one job. The old man was creaking at the joints and couldn't go on forever.

Now, as Gregg stood on the board-walk stamping the kinks from his suit, his eyes settled on the poster pinned up outside the telegraph office.

ALBERTO CORDOZA'S
GRAND CIRCUS
WILL VISIT GILBEY'S MEADOW
ADJACENT TO NELLY'S NIPPLE
WEEK COMMENCING JUNE 12
PERFORMANCES 3.30 AND 8 PM
Admittance: One dollar for grown
persons, fifty cents for children
A FEROCIOUS LION WILL FIGHT
A GRIZZLY BEAR
(THE VICTORIOUS ANIMAL WILL
HAVE FIREWORKS PLACED ON
HIS BACK WHICH WILL PRODUCE
ENTERTAINING AMUSEMENT)
LULU THE TATTOOED LADY
ZOLA'S HIGH WIRE ACT

# ACROBATS . . .
## PERFORMING ANIMALS . . .
### BRASS BAND

Gregg grunted with disgust. Sounded as if those animals were in for a rough time, and he'd never favored maltreating dumb beasts — unless they were for eating. None the less, he reckoned he'd get along to see the show and maybe take Marie-Belle if she could persuade Lucy May to give her a night off, which wouldn't be easy for she was one of the most popular of the soiled doves. And he knew why, because she could give a man all he needed, and more. He'd once told her, he hoped to take her away from that way of life and make her a respectable woman. Maybe when he stepped into Aaron's boots. And, at the time, he'd meant what he'd said.

But right now, he had other things to consider. Firstly, he went to his lodgings, took off his fancy suit and had an all-over wash. Next, he adorned his more comfortable working clothes, buckled on his gun and reported in at the marshal's office. He found Aaron, looking like the frazzled end of a misspent life, slumped in his chair, drawing on the stub of a cigarette, with a great bandage around his head. An empty beef stew can was in front of him.

'You never eat a decent meal,' Gregg said. 'Everythin' out of a can, all the time. Wonder your belly don't cut up a shine. Anyway, what hit you, Aaron?'

Aaron grunted with annoyance. He dropped his cigarette stub into the empty can where it sizzled and expired. He wiped gravy from his cookie-duster with the back of his hand and in a flat, somewhat shameful voice related the events of the previous night. The truth was he felt right sick at the death of the undertaker and the way he himself had been out-foxed by a bunch of cowboys.

He touched his bandaged head. 'I got a bump the size of an egg up there. It's sittin' alongside the bump Hilda gave me when she hit me with a fryin' pan.'

Gregg listened with a dismayed shake of his sandy head. 'What she do that for?'

'She said I was stoned.' Aaron allowed himself a wistful thought about the female who had been his wife for so many years.

'Were you stoned?'

'I couldn't say,' Aaron grunted. 'But I had a hell of a hangover when I woke up next mornin'.'

It was funny how it was only nowadays that he realized how much he'd loved Hilda.

He changed the subject back to the present. 'Reckon we'll have to ride out to *The Golden Rooster* and arrest Billy Cameron.'

'His daddy ain't gonna take too kindly to that,' Gregg said.

'Well, whatever he thinks, Lyle Cameron ain't the law in this territory, despite the fact that he runs his cowpokes like a private army. Gregg, we'll leave at daybreak tomorrow, do what's got to be done.'

'Daybreak?' Gregg queried. 'Didn't think you got up that early.'

'Well, just after daybreak.'

Gregg nodded. 'Aaron . . . you better make out your last will and testament tonight, just in case.'

★ ★ ★

The piebald mare was a hell-fire nag. She'd try to corner you in her stall, so that she could bite and kick. Her usual greeting was to flatten her ears back and bare her teeth, with the whites of her caustic eyes showing. She would buck and pitch like a half-broken bronc with veins full of snake-blood, and often Aaron would leave her standing saddled, letting her 'soak' for a while, before he took her out. He dreaded the day when she learned roll-overs. She was aptly named 'Mockey'.

Folks had asked Aaron so many times why he kept her. He'd tell them that for some crazy reason he was attached to her because she reminded him of Hilda, although he couldn't point to exactly how — unless it was the way the mare curled her lip and snarled. Or maybe it was because he couldn't tell which was uglier: her front or rear end. He'd had the same problem with Hilda.

Anyway, by ten o'clock next morning he'd shucked off his blankets, saddled and cinched-up the piebald and he and Gregg Mason were setting out for *The Golden Rooster*. Aaron as if he were a damned Apache with the bandage wound about his head like a turban. It made his hat perch high on his pate. His headache was akin to a hangover, in which he was well experienced. Both men packed artillery, though as usual Aaron hoped he wouldn't have to use his Colt, because his trigger finger had stiffened of late with rheumatism. In the old days, mind you, he'd been pretty handy when it came to gunplay.

Gregg always fancied his chances and spent hours in practice, firing at Aaron's empty cans and honing his draw. He'd filed down his pistol's mechanism so it would go off at the slightest touch. On one occasion he'd splattered a sidewinder at fifty yards.

Aaron knew damned well that bringing in Billy Cameron would be no easy matter. Lyle, his father, had accrued immense wealth with his cattle empire, but he had also accrued hate. He was an intimidating man, shaping life to his own design, hard on humans and animals alike.

Way back, Lyle Cameron had been one of the first ranchers to see the potential of the vast prairies stretching east of the fledgling town of Nelly's Nipple. Here, with superb grazing, a temperate climate and groves of shading trees, was perfect cattle country. As the Indian Wars flared, numerous military posts were built to protect the trails and an immense demand arose to satisfy the meat-hungry Army. The drives overland were perilous, but the subsequent sale of fleshy beeves at exorbitant prices had brought Lyle Cameron a fortune. His cowboys had lynched and shot rustlers with such savagery that the survivors had turned to safer crimes. He had crushed any competitors that stood in his way, brutally driving out homesteaders who built their hovels on his land. In due course the military markets had been supplemented by demands from Indian reservations, bringing even greater profit.

It was common knowledge how Lyle Cameron had had the lower part of his left leg blown off by a ball from a Napoleon 12-pounder at the battle of Spotsylvania in 1864, but with a stout wooden leg, he had subsequently proved himself as mobile and as good a horseman as anybody. But the injury had twisted his mind and he held a grudge against all mankind — apart from his son Billy. He doted on him.

# 4

The sun had turned into a brassy ball as the marshal and his deputy rode under the decorated gold-colored archway that rose starkly against the blue sky, its lettering proclaiming that they were entering land belonging to *The Golden Rooster*. The trail beckoned them onward and all around, the land rose and fell like gentle waves in a green ocean, punctuated here and there with sun-glinting streams, Saguaro cactus, prickly pear and ridges lined with cedar. To Aaron, this place seemed like the top of the world, with canyons draining away at the sides. Much to Mockey's agitation, a rattlesnake, disturbed by vibration of the ground, set up its angry buzzing sound and reluctantly shifted from the trail as they approached. Cattle were scattered about, mostly Herefords, grazing on the succulent grasses.

A half-hour later, they spotted three riders, blocking the trail ahead, holding their horses in, the sun glinting on gun metal.

It seemed they'd been expected.

They continued relentlessly, coming up the gentle rise in the trail to confront the cowboys. There, they reined in.

Aaron recognized the welcoming committee — the split-lipped Will Brosker in his bright red bandanna, simple-brained but mean, hatchet-nosed Jake Simpson whose eyes were so close-set he could look through a keyhole with both at once. The marshal's pulse quickened as he noticed the third man, hanging back slightly. Seth Cranshaw, the fella who'd thrown the bottle. No wonder he was hiding behind the others.

'We've come to speak with Lyle Cameron,' Aaron drawled, keeping his voice low-key.

Brosker removed a cigarette stub

from his lips, tossed it away. 'Well he sure don't wanna see you.'

'We weren't expectin' no warm hospitality,' Aaron remarked dryly. 'Now, if you'll pull to the side and let us through, I'd be obliged.'

None of the three moved.

'And there's something else,' Aaron went on, turning his attention to Seth Cranshaw. 'I'm chargin' you with throwin' a bottle at me. Obstructin' the law is a serious offense, that and wastin' good whiskey.'

'No point in chargin' me, Marshal,' Cranshaw responded. 'I been nowhere near Nelly's Nipple for weeks. You must be referin' to my twin brother.'

Aaron grunted with annoyance, took a closer look at Cranshaw. He'd forgotten about the Cranshaw twins. They seemed to inter-change to suit their own convenience. It was difficult to pin either of them down.

'Well, we'll sort that out later on,' Aaron said. 'Now kindly let us through, or I'll charge you all with obstructin' the law. I'll get the County Sheriff in, if I have to.'

Will Brosker laid his hand on the stock of his Remington Repeater. 'Like I said, Marshal, you ain't welcome here. Lyle don't wanna waste no time talkin' to you.'

'Talkin' about murder ain't time wastin',' Aaron said.

Jake Simpson had angled his sorrel off to the side, as if he expected lead to start flying. The situation was suddenly taut as a drum. For a second the only sound was the buzz of a big bluebottle that fussed about the horses' heads.

'You threatenin' us?' Deputy Gregg Mason enquired.

'Nope,' Brosker said. 'It's jes' your hosses we'll gun down, that's if you don't turn around and go home.'

'We come to do a job,' Aaron insisted. 'If you don't back off, we'll take you all in for obstructin' the law. And I'll make damn sure you get the maximum sentence.'

'*Ha!*' Will Brosker forced a humorless

laugh, his face red like his bandanna as the tension rose in him. 'You've asked for this, Marshal. Seems that horsemeat you're ridin' is evil anyway.'

Aaron sensed what was coming. He yanked hard at his reins and jerked Mockey to the side as Brosker's Springfield blasted off, the lead missing the piebald's head by a whisker's breadth, setting the beast rearing in panic.

Meanwhile, Gregg had drawn his Colt, blazed off to splinter the stock of Brosker's repeater, wrenching it clean out of his grasp and somehow unseating the cowboy from his saddle. His big bay horse was off like a rocket, dragging his erstwhile rider over the rough ground by his stirrup-hooked foot. Into the reverberation of the gunfire came the blueness of cursing and the alarmed whinnying of the other horses as they pranced in alarm. Mockey had launched into a regular dance, switching ends, rearing and kicking out with her rear hoofs, but Aaron was holding on and he gradually brought her under control.

He cast a glance in the direction that Brosker had taken, saw how he had now disentangled himself from the alarmed bay and was sitting in the grass nursing his injured ankle and looking downright sorry for himself. When Aaron turned back, he saw how Gregg was covering Jake Simpson and Cranshaw with his Colt. Both men were keeping their hands well clear of their hardware.

Aaron felt real proud of the way he'd taught Gregg to handle himself.

'You two,' Gregg was saying, 'clear out while you got the chance, and don't tangle with the law again!' He waved his gun as if he was anxious for more target practice.

Simpson and Cranshaw exchanged glances, then Simpson nodded his head and simultaneously they turned their animals and spurred them into motion, moving off the trail. Within seconds they were hightailing into the distance, not even stopping to comfort the fallen Brosker, who was only now hobbling to his feet.

Twenty minutes later, and without experiencing further trouble, the two lawmen allowed their horses to refresh themselves in a river. The water, slightly gypsum-tainted, created a faint sulphurous odor. Afterwards, they forded the river, passing through bulrushes and clumps of wild rose, to approach the vast swale that led to Cameron's formidable *Golden Rooster* ranch house.

# 5

The place had expanded considerably since Aaron's last visit. Cameron's empire clearly had gone from strength to strength, as it had expanded to encompass all the land between the Hathaway Mountains and the Carlos River, an area as big as a county. On the eastern side of the fine white-painted house were six bunk-houses, indicating the large numbers of hired hands that were taken into employ — a private army, as Aaron called it. He figured that if the Texas Rangers or US Cavalry stormed the place, they'd unearth more outlaws than were in any other part of the country. Most of them were so crooked, they'd chew nails and spit out corkscrews. Cameron favored hiring hard men to ensure that it was his word that ruled the roost.

The house boasted a broad porch.

Behind the living accommodation were the peeled-log ramblings of the hayricks, the feed and foaling sheds and stables. All the buildings were in the lee of a knoll so as to escape the fury of the cold winter winds, but right now the afternoon was as hot as a burnt boot.

The two visitors were observed with hostile eyes as they approached the house, men in scarred leather chaps pausing as they forked hay, groomed horses, carried out other chores. A group of children stood in the shadow of a barn, watching the lawmen as if fascinated. Down in the corrals, some calves were being branded, their alarmed mooing sounding, the smell of singeing flesh tainting the air. Aaron glanced about for Billy Cameron, but concluded he wouldn't be standing around waiting to be arrested.

The lawmen drew rein in front of the wide steps that led up to the porch of the house, and the first indication that they were expected came with the slow creak of a rocking chair. Gazing into the shadows beneath the balcony, they saw the barrel-chested figure of Lyle Cameron, gently working his rocker with downward pressure of his wooden leg against the porch boards. A Springfield rifle rested across his knees.

Cameron's head was hairless; so was his face. Now his gaze seized onto his visitors, burning with an intensity that was akin to madness.

'Good day, Lyle,' Aaron drawled. 'We wanna talk to you about your boy.'

Cameron ceased his rocking, his tongue darting from his mouth to wet his lips. 'Talk then!'

'Could sure do with some refreshment after ridin' through the heat,' Aaron said.

'None available,' Cameron responded. 'You wanna talk about my boy, then talk an' be on your way. I ain't got all day to sit here.'

'Lyle,' Aaron said, 'your boy Billy shot Silas Fogwell dead on Saturday night. I come to take him in.'

Cameron snorted with contempt.

'Well, Billy ain't around right now.'

Aaron heard the jingle of spurs and was aware that some cowboys had moved in to stand behind them.

'The killin' was self defense,' Cameron said, his deep voice coming slowly.

'That'll be for a judge to decide,' Aaron commented.

'It'll be for me to decide,' Cameron said. 'And I already decided. It was self defense. Now get off my land before I have you thrown off.'

Aaron shifted position in his saddle, easing his aching limbs. Gregg remained silent, his eyes darting around, watching for the first sign of violence.

'You're obstructin' the law, Lyle,' Aaron said. 'It's my duty to take Billy in, an' I'm gonna do it one way or other.'

'If you want a quiet life in that town o' yours,' Cameron said, 'then forget about Billy. You should know that sometimes I just can't control my men, especially when they go skally-hootin' into town. If they start drinkin', they get awful mean. Now, I ain't got anymore to say.' He clamped his jaw shut like he was biting the sights off a six-gun.

In all, this reinforced the marshal's prior opinion that Cameron wasn't, nor ever would be, the kind of fella you'd want to discuss the weather with.

Aaron nodded bleakly. He was truly riled but it didn't show. He knew that right now there was nothing he could do, but he wasn't going to be browbeaten by this man. He exchanged a nod with Gregg and as they turned their horses, forcing the group of cowboys to step aside, he gave Cameron his final word.

'I'll see you in court, Lyle.'

★ ★ ★

They were half way back to town, the sun's heat slackening, when the shots boomed out — heavy caliber rifle fire that burned the air close to their ears, too near for comfort. Aaron had been thinking about what he could do next to bring Billy Cameron to justice, but suddenly all thoughts were banished from his mind apart from the blind instinct to survive. Both Mockey and Gregg's sorrel were rearing in panic, but while Gregg kept in his saddle, Aaron lost his grip and he was pitched off, briefly aware of flying through the air before he thudded to the earth on his back, the sickening thud jarring every ounce of air from his body, both ends.

*I've broken my back*, he thought.

He fought for his breath, shock waves running through him, but somehow he got his lungs functioning once more. He lay gazing up into the sky, could see the clouds floating around, peering down at him like the stupid, empty things they were.

He wondered if more shooting was about to erupt. He was the next step up from a 'sitting' target — a 'lying' target, or was it a 'laying' target. He could never work out the difference between lying and laying, one having to do with telling untruths and the other to do with the production of eggs. But he guessed his mind was getting addled. Silence flowed about him, silence that was gradually broken by the receding pound of hoofs as Mockey high-tailed into the distance. It was crazy — silence being broken by something that was growing fainter, but that was the way it seemed. Damn that mare, he thought.

Maybe he'd shoot her after all, that was if he ever survived to get to his feet again.

The thud of more hoofs was vibrating the ground. It was Gregg turning his sorrel. A moment later, he was dismounting and dropping to his knees alongside his boss.

'You all right, Aaron?'

Aaron grunted with impatience. 'Do I look all right? I'm dyin' with a broken back!'

'Well, sit up then, while you're still alive.'

He stood behind Aaron, hooked his

hands under his armpits and yanked him into a sitting position. Aaron unleashed a yowl, then his cussing scorched the air.

'Broken back be damned,' Gregg said.

The marshal worked his shoulders, flexed his arms. He looked sheepish. 'Well, it sure felt broken.' He glanced around anxiously. 'Them shots came mighty close.'

'Yeah,' Gregg nodded, 'I guess it was some of Cameron's cowboys tryin' to scare us off. Shots came from that low ridge over yonder. We best get back to town before they try it again. That dawgone mare o' yours is long gone. You'll have to climb up behind me.'

Reluctantly, Aaron nodded. The whole business was downright humiliating. He gingerly allowed Gregg to drag him into a standing position, cursing at the pain in his back.

'Where've my teeth gawn?' he said. 'They must've jumped out.'

Gregg searched fruitlessly around.

'God knows,' he said. 'You're better off without them.'

A moment later they were continuing their journey to town. Eventually, when he walked into his office, he made a discovery. Sitting on his desk, grinning at him, were his teeth. Damn it, he'd forgotten to put them in after breakfast.

# 6

Next morning, Emily Grapewrath, wife of the Reverend Grapewrath, held her monthly meeting of the Town Women's Guild & Temperance Society. The Guild's activities included debates, lectures, group singing and the condemnation of liquor, as well as dealing with matters of social importance, such as discouraging the use of profane language within the town's confines.

Mrs. Grapewrath was an angular, bony woman. Her eyes were the color of a bleak autumn sky and matched the dress she wore. Eight other ladies, women who considered themselves of good class, were in attendance, sitting around the long table in the upstairs room of the Methodist Church, looking immensely prim in their high-buttoned dresses and straw boaters, the latter, with blue ribbons, having become the accepted uniform of Guild members.

They listened as Emily told them how the new silk-culture movement was sweeping across the West. Women everywhere were being drawn into it with hopes of earning enormous fortunes for good deeds and worthy charities. Apparently one acre planted with mulberry trees could yield enough to feed a million silk worms that, in turn, would produce four-hundred pounds of raw silk. This could be sold for $3000. Furthermore, a certain Mary Davidson of Junction City had written a manual for beginners.

However, Emily sensed a certain lack of interest among her listeners and she knew the reason why. They were just filling in time before the main business of the day.

Emily considered that included in today's agenda was an item of the utmost importance, certainly the most challenging issue the Guild had had to face during its short history. A significant guest was due to attend at

11 o'clock. Not that his presence would be greatly appreciated by the ladies, for he represented the lowest morality. The ladies had only recently grown to accept the crudity of the name of their town, Nelly's Nipple, but the latest development was truly obnoxious and a stand had to be made.

Now, as the wall-clock proclaimed that the appointed hour had arrived, there was a knock on the door, and the diminutive Mrs. Poindexter, the bank president's wife, rose to admit the visitor, the ladies murmuring their 'good mornings' as was befitting.

Bent Nose Beecher, proprietor of the saloon *Porky's Pride* stepped into the room, accepting the chair that Emily Grapewrath gestured him to. He was a well built man and might have been handsome had it not been for his lopsided nose. He was wearing a string tie and one of his brightly-colored silk waistcoats across which a gold watch chain hung. He had a good eye for business and a particular appetite for notoriety. His cough reflected a slight apprehension; after all to be confronted by such a formidable group of women was awesome. He guessed they all had blue wallpaper in their homes. But then he coughed again with much more determination. His face assumed a stubborn expression.

Mrs. Grapewrath cleared her throat and in her most formal manner said, 'Thank you for attending today, Mr. Beecher, and for arriving promptly.'

He didn't reply beyond a slight dip of his forehead. He was heavily outnumbered but he was ready for a fight.

Emily now spoke forcefully, the other women making small sounds of approval as she progressed. 'Mr. Beecher, we know that you are new to this town and may not be aware of the sort of behavior that has been established here — and the sort of things that are *not* acceptable.'

Again the slight dip of his head.

'Many townsfolk did not want your saloon to open, but we eventually took solace in the fact that all sins — drinking, gambling, bawdy behavior and . . . the pandering to men's lewd and wicked ways — would be combined under one roof. We hoped that decency would have a better chance of prevailing elsewhere. But you have provoked a very unsavory situation. We are particularly concerned for the sensitivity of our children.'

Bent Nose Beecher at last broke his silence. 'Will you please get to the point, Mrs. Grapewrath! I got to get back to work.'

The minister's wife opened her primped mouth to speak but closed it again, changing her mind about her next words. She was not used to being addressed so brusquely.

'Very well,' she eventually said. 'You know that it is the mural of the pig that disgusts us. Rearing up alongside the doorway to your establishment, displaying its huge . . . you know what! It's quite unnecessary. Such displays should be confined to the privacy of the hog-pen. All we ask is that you take it down and replace it with something more sightly and decent.'

'Yes!' The baker's wife had been fidgeting, anxious to speak her piece. 'Its private parts are totally out of proportion.'

There was a collective gasp from the assembled ladies. The matter was highly embarrassing.

Bent Nose Beecher rested his thick hand on the tabletop, his gold-ringed fingers drumming slightly as he collected his thoughts. After a moment he said, 'Porky's private parts ain't out of proportion. They're quite normal for pigs. The painting was made from life. He belongs to a farmer, a friend of mine, down at Fallow Springs. And furthermore . . . ' He hesitated, debating in his mind various complications. He reached a conclusion. 'Furthermore, I'll have him brought up here so you can see that picture's true to life . . . '

'No!' Esther Brown, the schoolmaster's wife, exclaimed. She looked pale, as if about to faint.

'I insist,' Beecher said. 'You have made an accusation that Porky's private parts are out of proportion. That is insultin'. Not only to the pig, but to the male sex generally.'

Grace Clapp, the doctor's wife, who was a big woman possessing certain porcine features herself, said, 'There is no pig on earth that looks that way. I think we should refer the matter to Aaron McLean. He's paid to keep the town respectable.'

There was a nodding of boaters, a general murmuring of acquiescence. With some reluctance, even Emily Grapewrath condescended.

Bent Nose Beecher smiled almost smugly, smoothing his lop-sided nose with his forefinger. If these busy-bodies wanted to go the whole hog, then so be it.

'Very well, ladies,' he said, 'You have made a scathin' accusation. I'll have Porky imported to Nelly's Nipple. At least that'll prove the point, so to speak!

51

You'll see that he has every right to be proud of his pighood.'

Emily Grapewrath could scarcely contain her anger. As she took a sip of water, her hand was trembling noticeably.

'Mr. Beecher.' Emotion gave her voice a bitter edge. 'If that pig appears in this town, I cannot guarantee that somebody will not castrate him — and I'm sure that whoever does the deed will have the full support of the marshal.'

Bent Nose Beecher did not delay. He rose to his feet, gave a curt nod to Emily Grapewrath, said, 'Good day, ladies,' and took his leave.

In the small hours of the following night, an unknown person threw a number of eggs at Porky's mural, leaving a messy splattering for the saloon proprietor to have wiped clean next morning. He figured he'd better recruit the assistance of Marshal Aaron McLean before those so-called ladies appealed to him for support.

# 7

Aaron lay face down upon a bed, his bruised back bared. Lucy May had the most loving touch. Her fingers moved up and down his spine as softly as a goose feather, her lips making gentle cooing sounds and telling him he shouldn't make a habit of falling off his horse, not at his age. To the side, her little poodle dog Maxine sat on a cushion and watched, her large dewy eyes following every movement of her mistress's hands.

'You say that mare came back to town under her own steam?' Lucy May enquired.

'Sure she did. Back in her stall when I got home. Didn't spare a thought for me. Damned bunch-quitter!'

'And you're going to shoot her?'

'Naw,' he sighed. 'Guess I couldn't do that.'

She smiled. She knew he loved that animal despite its ornery nature. Underneath his beans and mettle, he was as soft as half-churned butter.

Her thumbs employed a slight pressure to his back where special need was required. Presently she applied a liniment made from dried flower heads of arnica. This flooded the small room with the sweetest aroma.

Lucy May, who had an educated thirst and loved expensive champagne, had always provided her girls with an umbrella of protection, spread, as they had been, throughout the side streets of Nelly's Nipple. But now they were all under one roof at *Porky's Pride* and Bent Nose Beecher had furnished them with cozy upstairs accommodation, she was able to care for her chicks like a proud mother hen, ensuring that they were always clean, sweetly perfumed, wore elegant dresses and the finest lingerie. Not that Lucy May had the proportions of a mother hen, for she retained her petite and delectable figure even though she was now well into her forties. It was said she resembled the actress Lillie Langtry. She had the same creamy complexion, impudent blue eyes and slightly fading blonde curls piled high upon her head.

She had consoled Aaron for years, having made up for the lack of wifely comforts matrimony brought him — in fact ever since Hilda, in a fit of pique, had thrown his clothes, boots, spurs and other worldly possessions into the street from her bedroom window and left him to scrabble around in the all-together to restore his dignity. Hilda had said she didn't want kids because it wasn't fair on a woman. If a cow got pregnant, it was allowed to graze for a month so as to rest, but a woman was expected to cook and clean right up until she gave birth, not that Hilda herself had ever excelled at cooking and cleaning. She'd always said that it was only Aaron who made the place dirty and had kept him outside as far as possible. Anyway, she said, birth was a messy business, downright unladylike, and she didn't want to take any chance of getting in the family way. That accounted for her being as cold towards him as a polar bear's tit.

Now his formidable spouse was gone, Lucy May had formed an attachment to the Town Marshal that went beyond professionalism. He knew he could talk to her in a way he couldn't to anybody else. She'd even offered to do his washing, but to avoid troubling her he usually made do with 'hand-and-spit' laundry.

'It grieves me,' he confided, 'that Billy Cameron is gettin' away with murder. His brain cavity wouldn't make a drinkin' cup for a canary, but he knows he can hide anywhere out there on his pa's spread, 'specially with Lyle's cowboys protectin' him. We ain't never had trouble like this before.'

She began to work her thumbs into the painful knots of his neck and shoulders and he wasn't enjoying it so much, but he knew it loosened things up so he suffered in silence.

'I reckon Billy'll show up one o' these days,' she said, 'but watch out in the meantime because he's got a hell-fire temper. And his pa's meaner than a polecat with a burr under his tail.'

'Yeah, he'd eat off the same plate as a snake.' He unleashed an anguished sigh. He decided to turn his mind to nicer things.

He reached into his pocket and took out a glass bead necklace. Nigh fifteen year ago he'd bought it from a carpetbagger salesman for good money and given it to Hilda on her birthday, but she'd thrown it in the trash bin. He'd recovered it, stowed it away. Now he gave it to Lucy May, fitting it around her slim neck. She looked at herself in a side mirror and smiled with pleasure.

'Hilda didn't care for it,' he said, 'so I'd like you to have it. She said it was cheap rubbish.'

'So it is. But it's the thought that counts. It's real thoughtful of you to give it to me, especially as it holds memories of Hilda for you.'

They laughed together. They often laughed together, sometimes at nothing.

'Lucy May,' he whispered. 'I guess it's time for nookie. I've taken off my spurs.'

'Wouldn't do your back no good.'

'Don't play hard to get,' he chuckled. 'It's not natural for you. Your name's Lucy May, not Lucy May Not.'

Her voice became dreamy, the way he loved it. 'For a fella your age, you're as frisky as a puppy.'

'Why don't you admit it. You enjoy it as much as I do.'

Maxine the poodle settled down on her cushion and curled up. She'd seen it all before.

'You're special, Aaron,' Lucy May murmured, her lips touching his ear, and after that they didn't talk for a while.

★   ★   ★

Aaron figured that if Hilda had still been around, she'd have been a leading light in the Town Women's Guild & Temperance Society. In fact she would have rivaled the sky pilot's wife for the leadership — and for certain she'd have been up front in the procession of ladies, all in straw boaters, who paraded along main street a couple of mornings later, holding their placards aloft, proclaiming. PORKY OUT ... NO TO PORKY ... PORKY IS AN INSULT TO OUR CHILDREN.

Mrs. Grapewrath led the strident chanting, emphasizing their demands. Storekeepers stood in their doorways, amused, as the procession marched by and several dogs barked in unison, seeming to empathize with the ladies. Nothing like this had ever been seen in Nelly's Nipple.

The minister's wife led the way to the saloon. Below its porch, they stopped, a phalanx of indignation. They were standing directly before the hated, life-sized mural, some of them lowering their eyes, rather than look at the object of their disgust. Those who found the courage to take a peep were even more shocked, for they swore afterwards that the animal was grinning directly at them, seemingly exultant in his blatant nudity.

Meanwhile several barkeeps, sweepers up, Violette La Plante and other girls, some in silk gowns, leaned against the porch rail and directed insults at the demonstrators, telling them to mind their own business, but this achieved little, apart from attracting surprisingly uncharacteristic and abusive language from ladies who should have known better. So bitter was their tirade, that Emily Grapewrath was obliged to restrain them.

The situation rose to a climax when two of the barkeeps dragged out a hose, pump and fire buckets from the rear of the premises and, amid much laughter, sent a spume of water over the red faced ladies, cooling their ardor no end and turning them back down the street in some disarray.

Aaron arrived on the scene, having only recently quit his bunk in the cell, just in time to satisfy himself that order had been restored.

It was notable that Bent Nose Beecher, the saloon proprietor, was not present. He had in fact gone to Fallow Springs to collect Porky. Deputy Gregg Mason had accompanied him to act as escort. Beecher felt certain that a real live pig, particularly one of such large proportions, would add color to his establishment, furthering his aim to spread the saloon's notoriety and attract clients from far beyond Nelly's Nipple, and completely falsifying the claim of the Guild ladies that the mural was out of proportion. They would see that it was simply a representation of Porky as God had created him.

★   ★   ★

Round about two o'clock that afternoon Bent Nose Beecher and Gregg

Mason got back from Fallow Springs, riding on a canvas-topped wagon drawn by two mules. The vehicle weighed heavily on wheels that creaked as if with aches and pains caused by the heavy burden. As progress was made along Main Street towards the saloon, folks gathered on the boardwalks and watched with some awe, but they could see nothing of the wagon's cargo, for the flaps were tied down and fastened. Bent Nose Beecher had a satisfied smile on his lips.

# 8

As he fumbled with the makings of a smoke, Aaron watched from his office. He was still feeling downright sore about his failure to bring Billy Cameron to justice. It rankled him that the stump-legged rancher and his buck-toothed, no-good son should get the better of him and he raked his brain to come up with some solution, but to no avail. His thinking altered course as he saw the wagon go past and he exchanged a wave with his young deputy.

Leaving a deep set of grooves in the street's dust, the wagon turned down the side alley leading to the back of *Porky's Pride* and passed from view.

Presently Aaron saw Bent Nose leave the saloon and walk towards the office, and he guessed he was shortly to have a visitor — and visitors usually meant trouble.

Beecher stepped inside, beating the dust from his fancy suit. His watch chain looked tarnished and his silk waistcoat was damp with the sweat of driving the wagon through searing heat.

'Aaron,' he said brusquely, 'I've brought Porky to town to prove to them stuck up females that he's just a normal animal, and that there ain't no difference between his pecker and any other pig's pecker.'

'Sure,' Aaron drawled, 'but since you been away the Woman's Guild have demonstrated with placards and shoutin'. Them women were sure riled up. They had to be hosed down to cool them off.'

Bent Nose chuckled. 'I heard. I wish I'd seen it. But I won't be browbeaten by narrow mindedness. So called 'righteous females' can be downright dangerous, and they've threatened violence against that pig, and he ain't done nothing to deserve that. He's just a simple, law-abidin' pig.'

'Tell me,' Aaron said, 'when you've proved your point, or rather Porky's point. When you've proved he ain't out of proportion, are you gonna take him back to Fallow Springs?'

Beecher shook his head. 'I sure ain't! I paid good money for that pig, and he's gonna be a permanent fixture at the saloon.'

'You mean mix with the customers?' Aaron asked.

'Sure. He'll be a real novelty.'

'But won't he . . . you know? All over the place, I mean.'

'Pigs are clean animals, Aaron. They can be trained to shit at the proper time and place.'

'You mean in the privy?'

'In the hog-pen.'

'Oh.'

'But we're gettin' off the subject. What I came to say was that I fear for the safety of that pig, and I want to have a guard mounted on his pen, 'specially at night. I'll pay for whatever services you can provide. Maybe you could get some volunteers and work out a roster.'

'Fellas may not be willin' to give up a night's sleep,' Aaron said.

'Oh, I reckon they will. You see menfolk feel threatened by this situation. They feel the male sex is being victimized by a load of prissy women and they won't stand for it. Gregg Mason understands the situation, says he'll gladly take his turn, and there are a lot of others too.'

Aaron drew on his cigarette, nodded. He didn't like the way things were brewing up. A murder of the town's undertaker was hard enough to handle, but a civil war between women and men was something he'd never considered. The whole town would have to take one side or the other. He couldn't lock up the entire population for breaking the peace. After all, he only had the one cell, and he needed that to sleep in himself.

'Will you help?' Beecher persisted.

Aaron shuffled his feet awkwardly.

He felt overtaxed.

'I'll . . . do what I can,' he mumbled.

'Good,' Beecher nodded. 'Now how about steppin' across and seein' Porky for yourself, seeing how he ain't near so bad as them women are makin' out?'

The thought of visiting a pig, a woosher, paying his respects to the town's new celebrity, amused Aaron.

'Sure,' he said, reaching for his hat.

He followed Beecher out of his office. They walked down the street and took the alley at the side of the saloon. A moment later and they were peering over the hog-pen wall. Aaron was impressed by what he saw. Beecher had clearly put some thought into having the pen built. Aaron doubted that any pig had previously had such a grand structure to live in. It was spacious, made of good timber. In one corner was a well-watered mud-patch. There was plenty of straw scattered around, a big trough and a doorway leading to the living section that was nicely shadowed, providing complete privacy and protection from the elements.

'Pigs can get real bad sunburn if they're not protected,' Beecher commented. 'That's why they wallow in mud, to shield their skin. It's their sort of beauty treatment.'

Aaron nodded. 'Where *is* the beasty?' he enquired, speaking in a hushed voice as if they were in the presence of royalty.

'I'll let him know he's got visitors.' Beecher place two fingers between his lips and unleashed a loud whistle.

There was a delayed response from within the shelter, a deep sigh, then a sort of rumbling and grunting sound, an indication of heavy weight being raised — and then, out of the shadows, the great pig appeared, practically filling the doorway, wheezing, his ears perked. He was clearly indicating the porcine equivalent of, 'Yeah, whatcha want?'

Porky's main color was black, but his shoulders and stumpy forelegs were pink, as if he was wearing a long-sleeved vest. His muck-caked, bristly hide looked as tough as armor-plating and he had a fearsome set of teeth. Aaron felt relieved that his adult incisor tusks had been cut back.

Porky now chose to move forward on his sure-footed, cloven trotters. He approached the wall of the pen and thrust his moist snout at Aaron, who patted him. He admired the pig's dainty eye-lashes, just as fine as those possessed by some of the saloon girls. And he thought how good Porky's snout must be for levering and digging. He could do with such an appendage himself, for sifting through evidence.

'If you were a lady,' Beecher said, 'he'd give you a kiss. He's a real friendly critter. He'll bring customers from far and wide, you'll see.'

*If he survives*, Aaron thought. At that moment he felt a distinct dislike for certain members of the female sex. The depiction in the mural was not an inch out of proportion, except in one respect.

'His privates are sure huge,' Aaron observed, 'but they don't seem quite so big as the painting shows,' Aaron observed.

Beecher coughed, seemed to ignore the comment. 'Despite his weight and short legs,' he said, 'he's a real fast runner. A cross between a Razorback and a New Hampshire hog, that's what he is. Furthermore, he can perform tricks.'

Aaron absorbed the information, but he was still troubled.

'His private parts don't seem so big as the painting shows,' he repeated. 'Mebbe the artist got carried away.

Beecher shrugged his shoulders. 'No,' he said. 'It's the wrong time of the day.'

Aaron wasn't so certain, but he gave Porky a farewell pat and the two men went through the back way into the saloon where Aaron partook of a large glass of milk, forgetting to wipe the cream from his cookie-duster.

True to his word, he mentioned the situation that evening to Lucy May, and she felt sure that quite a few of her clients would be pleased to volunteer for guard duty, being able to combine that chore with other pleasures. Protecting Porky would provide more credible excuses for absence than those they usually gave to their wives.

'That's if they can convince their women that it's a just cause,' Aaron said.

'Sure they will,' Lucy May smiled. 'Leave it to me.'

That night Gregg Mason stood guard at the hog-pen. By the following afternoon Lucy May had obtained a considerable list of volunteers and Aaron had drawn up a roster.

# 9

Aaron's reading skill was slow, like his drawling voice. Sometimes he followed the printed line with his finger. Today, he was studying Silas Fogwell's obituary in *The Nelly's Nipple News*. He was surprised that the man had been a gambler, successfully working the river boats between New Orleans and St. Louis, before taking up undertaking. *Taking up* undertaking! That sounded downright strange. Wouldn't *undertaking* undertaking be better? Come to think of it, that didn't sound so good either.

'Marshal, I noticed that Mr. Beecher visited you yesterday.'

He straightened up in his office chair and raised his eyes, startled by the abrupt comment. He found himself meeting the bleak autumnal gaze of Emily Grapewrath. Her face reminded him of a cow's face as it waited in line for a tic-dipping.

'He sure did, Ma'am,' he said, and though he didn't feel amiable towards the minister's wife, he added, 'Take a seat.'

'No thanks. What I've got to say won't take long. Mr. Beecher probably told you about the situation regarding the pig. At least his version of the situation.'

'Yup,' Aaron nodded.

'The fact is,' she went on, 'that animal is disgusting, and Mr. Beecher had no right to bring it here.'

Aaron put his hat over his false teeth; they were snarling at him from his desk top. 'He said he brought the pig in to prove that the life-sized paintin' wasn't out of proportion,' he explained.

'Well, no doubt you've seen the monster. No doubt you've seen it isn't nearly as big as that painting. At least not its private parts.'

Aaron absorbed her words.

'Anyway, Marshal, I warned Mr.

Beecher that if he brought that pig here, the only decent thing to do would be to get it castrated.'

'And what did he say to that?' Aaron knew the answer but he had to humor the woman.

She clicked her tongue with displeasure. 'I don't think he agreed.'

'Mrs. Grapewrath, I must tell you that there are a lot of menfolk in town who appreciate havin' Porky here. He's a sort of novelty and talkin' point. And they won't take kindly to that pig bein' threatened.'

'Yes, those roustabouts who frequent that doggery and indulge their evil drinking and womanizing. The whole thing's an insult to the good folks of this community. It'll make us the laughing stock of the whole country.'

'Hell, perhaps you're getting' this whole business out of proportion, Ma'am!'

'It's not me getting things out of proportion,' she bristled, clenching her fists. 'And watch your language, Marshal!'

Aaron tried a conciliatory approach. He dropped his voice a notch. 'Not that I'm sayin' I can't see your point of view.'

'Well in that case, you'll agree with me that Mr. Beecher has to be taught a lesson. And the best way to do that is to castrate the animal — either that or slaughter it. Which would you say is the best solution, castration or slaughter?'

'Well . . . that pig hasn't committed any crime, so far as we know. Slaughterin' it wouldn't seem fair . . .'

'So it's got to be castration, then,' she announced with some finality.

'But . . .'

'It'll have to be done privately.'

'A private job?' he queried.

'Exactly.'

Aaron shook his head doubtfully. 'I don't think the butcher will do it.'

'No he won't. I've already asked him.' She paused, then went on. 'Last Sunday, my husband preached on the licentious and evil ways of male creatures.'

'But surely,' Aaron argued, 'The Good Lord gave male creatures their needs, and put females in the world to satisfy them.'

'That's blasphemy, Aaron McLean!' she cried. 'Anyway, my husband appealed for money to bring propriety to this town. The response was overwhelming. I offered the proceeds to the butcher if he would help us, but he said he wouldn't do it. And that's why I've come you, Aaron. You want to maintain the good name of this town, although you don't always act as if you do. I understand pig castration's not major surgery.'

He felt flabbergasted. 'Now hold on, Ma'am. Castration ain't part of my duty.'

'I was told you were a farmer before you studied law.'

He stayed quiet, refusing to be drawn. He hadn't been a great success as a farmer. The work had been too hard.

She went quite pale, waiting for him

to be more helpful, but he didn't oblige and eventually she lost her patience.

'Very well. I thought in coming to you, we'd be able to sort things out, but it seems the upholding of the law in Nelly's Nipple is seriously below standard. What with unpunished murder and . . . '

'Now hold on, Mrs. Grapewrath. That murder is another matter. Under investigation, it is.' He steadied his anger. 'Bent Nose Beecher and I discussed the pig. I've said I can see both sides of the argument. It seems to me we need some sort of mediator. Somebody who'll see both the male and female point of view. I'll volunteer. I'll consider all the evidence I can lay hands on and reach a decision.'

'You!' For a second he thought she'd explode. Her face had changed from the paleness of alabaster to rising scarlet. 'I can see now. You're as biased as the rest of those rabble raisers, as red blooded male as . . . '

'Ma'am, with respect, I'm too old

now to be classed as red blooded male.'

'That's not what I heard, Aaron McLean.'

He felt uncomfortable. What was she getting at?

'Heard from who?' he ventured.

'My husband told me what you're like with loose women. Frisky as a puppy, you are.'

Aaron was taken aback. He lowered his eyes, went quiet. Then a question loomed into his mind. 'How does your husband know that?'

She blustered about for a moment, then said, 'Oh those saloon girls told him. They told him exactly what you're like.'

'So the minister is a customer of them girls?'

'Not a customer, certainly not,' she cried indignantly. 'How can you suggest such a thing! The fact is their souls need saving more than anybody else's in town.'

'Oh sure,' he said.

'You think about what I've said,' she went on. 'You start considering what your duty is as a peace officer. Now I must be on my way.' She bobbed her straw-boater in a curt nod. 'Good day, Marshal.'

# 10

Feeling the rising tension in Nelly's Nipple, and concerned about his fruitless attempt to apprehend Billy Cameron, Aaron allowed himself a lay-in next morning. It was somewhere close to ten o'clock and he was on his prison-cell bunk, snoring fiercely, when an awesome noise shattered all restfulness. It sounded like hell emigrating on cartwheels; it scared the wits out of him. He had never heard anything like it. He wrestled clear of his blanket, pulling on his boots.

He stumbled through the office and peered into the street from his porch. If the sound had been awesome, the sight was even more so.

The air was bludgeoned by a cacophony blasting forth from a calliope, a big pin-and-barrel instrument, placed on a wagon, with a set of steam-powered brass whistles producing a sound more like a thundering locomotive than any musical rendition. The calliope-bearing wagon, drawn by two white plough-horses, was part of a parade that was stretching along Main Street. And now, supplementing the instrument's earbusting clamor, came the trumpeting of elephants and the roar of a lion.

Alberto Cardoza's Grand Circus had come to Nelly's Nipple.

A man who was clearly Alberto Cardoza himself led the way, looking like a Humpty Dumpty, with his egg-shaped body, huge girth, long black dreadlocks, blue striped suit and thigh-high wader boots. His top-hat was streaming with red ribbons, and he was constantly doffing it to the adults and excited, shouting children lining the street, and flashing his gold-toothed smile to all and sundry.

Following on, came two elephants, painted red and blue, finely bedecked and bearing baskets upon their backs

81

from which scantily clad ladies waved to the gathering crowd. Then came four camels, and a cage on wheels with a fierce looking lion peering through the bars. Every so often he unleashed a low rumble intensifying into a roar, which made the dust rise and had more than one town dog scampering down a back alley with his tail between his legs. Other cages followed, containing bears, dogs and other creatures, some clearly fresh from the wild. There was also a lady dressed as a fancy cowgirl, in divided skirt, fringes and boots, discharging her pistol into the air every so often.

The head of the procession came level with the saloon, and most of the hurdy-gurty girls and soiled doves were leaning over the porch rail to get a good view. With them, was Lucy May's poodle Maxine, yapping her head off. Also prominently on display was the saloon's greatest pride — Porky. The pig was bedecked in a fancy red cloak and cap, looking for all the world like the king of his castle surveying the kingdom. Rumor had it that the pig was already displaying exceptional skills for saloon customers, being able to bow to order, beg on his hind legs, shake hands and kiss compliant females. Positioned behind him, beaming with pride, was Bent Nose Beecher, resplendent in his waistcoat. Cardoza caught his eye, and strode over to him in animated fashion, reaching out to shake his hand. He then patted Porky's head with great affection, clearly lavishing praise, causing the pig to flutter his eye-lashes.

Aaron noticed how Cardoza's boot-clad legs were as stumpy as Porky's.

The circus man spoke at length to Beecher, gesturing towards the pig frequently, but such was the surrounding noise that even those standing close were unable to catch the gist of the conversation. Eventually Beecher gave his head a firm shake. Alberto Cardoza shrugged his fat shoulders somewhat despondently and scampered back to the procession, barking aggressive orders at his entourage as if to vent his feelings.

After the circus folk had passed through, Nelly's Nipple gradually slipped back to its tranquil normality and people trudged home.

The procession left behind a mess of churned up mud, a litter of handbills publicizing the forthcoming show — and several large dollops of elephant dung.

★　★　★

Alberto Cardoza's Grand Circus was not all *that* grand, although it had been one of the first to combine rail and boat travel with the hardship of long overland treks. It had spent four days on the trail to reach Nelly's Nipple. The day following the parade was one of feverish activity at Gilbey's Meadow, two miles out of town. The great central pole was erected and the canvas big-top hauled onto it. Lulu the tattooed lady, Giorgio the Lion King, Zola the velocipede rider, Zenobia who was to be fired from a cannon, numerous Siberian roller skaters as well as other performers, looking nothing like their celebrity status, shared the chores with laborers, tugging on ropes, blocks and pulleys and setting up equipment. All was under the scathing eye of Cardoza himself who had long since shed the greasy smiling manner he'd assumed during the parade. Now he cursed and insulted his underlings as they sweated, striding back and forth, whip in hand like an Egyptian slave driver.

The sun burned down and animals slumped, dispirited, in their cages; brown bears, lion, cougar, chimpanzee, monkeys. There was no shade for them and little water. Camels and horses were pegged out, dogs yapped incessantly, fighting bantams crowed, and occasionally Goliath the lion vented his frustration with a roar. Meanwhile a somewhat discordant brass band undertook rehearsal.

Next day the show commenced with open-air sharp-shooting competitions and exhibitions of balloon flying. Unwilling lambs were gleefully tied into baskets and dispatched into the heavens, and fireworks were let off. Cock fighting, 'pulling the chicken' and wild animal contests were staged, many bloody. Come early evening, the crowds of all ages and sexes flocked from town, squeezing into the big-top, all dressed in their best 'Sunday-go-to-meetin' clothes'. Such excitement, almost tangible, came rarely to dull lives on the Western Frontier.

But activity was not only confined to Gilbey's Meadow. Bent Nose Beecher had issued a written challenge to the ladies of Nelly's Nipple. He was inviting them to undertake a measuring ceremony. He believed this would refute their claim that the depiction of Porky's pecker on the mural was a travesty of reality. A further meeting of the Town Women's Guild & Temperance Society had been convened. It was agreed that the challenge would be taken up. It was suggested that Doctor

Clapp be asked to undertake the measuring, but his wife scoffed at this idea, saying he was nothing but a pill-roller and bound to be biased. Off handedly, she remarked that she would rather do it herself than ask him. This remark was immediately seized on as if it was a firm offer and after some delicate discussion, strait-laced Grace Clapp succumbed to persuasion to represent the Guild, eventually agreeing to attend such a ceremony, armed with her tape measure, at four o'clock next day. Mrs. Poindexter was nominated to accompany her for physical support. This seemed somewhat ludicrous, although nobody commented, as Mrs. Grace Clapp was a huge woman, built like a brick outhouse, while Peewee Poindexter was scarcely knee high to a grasshopper and skinny with it. However there was no doubt she could pack a punch if things turned ugly.

Emily Grapewrath felt certain that Bent Nose Beecher would be obliged to admit his mistake. After this, and barring immediate action on the saloon proprietor's part, she was determined to proceed with the pig's castration. The animal would then soon lose his lewd appeal and Beecher would be taught a lesson. She still firmly believed that Aaron McLean would carry out the surgical task, subject to adequate incentive being provided.

Secretly, she had to admit that she did not know what castration involved. She had never stooped to study the male private parts in any detail. Indeed both she and her minister husband had considered that carnal activity was sinful and depraved and therefore had never indulged. All she knew was that castration entailed the excision of certain parts and, in Porky's case, she hoped it would mean chopping the whole dangling monstrosity off, complete with any adjoining appendages.

# 11

As if representing both ends of the female size spectrum, Grace Clapp and Peewee Poindexter, caparisoned in their distinctive boaters, marched along Main Street and went where no woman had previously been, at least no woman of decent class — *Porky's Pride*. The faces of both Guild members were fixed with a dogged determination to get the job done, no matter how distasteful. At this time of the hot afternoon, everywhere appeared quiet and deserted, apart from the odd loafer, numerous families having ventured out to see the exhibitions at the circus grounds. Ignoring the lack of any hospitality, the two ladies stepped up onto the unhallowed boards of the saloon's porch, feeling that the fires of hell were licking at the soles of their shoes. Here was the place that lured men like slavering dogs circling around a bitch in heat.

Grace Clapp approached the mural, her face a picture of disgust, and fighting back nausea, measured the pig's male member, double-checking to ensure accuracy.

'Eight and a quarter inches,' she spat out, and Peewee Poindexter jotted the finding down in her note book.

The two ladies now ventured down the alley alongside the saloon to emerge at the small meadow where the hog-pen stood. Their nostrils quivered at the unmistakable smell of pig excrement.

This time they were greeted by Bent Nose Beecher, two of his apron-clad barkeeps, Violette La Plante, and her sister the dark-haired Mari Belle. They were waiting alongside the pen in readiness for what Beecher grandly called 'The Measuring Ceremony' and for any fun that might ensue. The nodded greetings from both parties lacked cordiality.

The ladies peered over the pen wall,

saw how the inside was covered in slurry and other despicable mess — but of the creature that had caused it all, there was no sight. Shortly, however, they became aware of snoring coming from within the shadowed shelter.

'Porky's dozin' right now,' Beecher explained. 'He won't be too pleased at being disturbed, but I'll call him out.'

He slid two fingers into his mouth and unleashed a whistle that had the ladies wincing with the shrillness — but their attention was distracted from expressing any complaint as Porky appeared, blinking his little eyes.

'Yeah, watcha want?' he would have said, had words come natural to him.

No doubt any answer he might have received would have embarrassed him to the core — unless, of course, he had seen the funny side of it. This appeared unlikely, for he now assumed an apprehensive and suspicious expression, his fierce teeth glinting in the sunlight.

The ladies gazed at the animal's

dangling appendage, their mouths sagging.

Beecher maintained a look of absolute solemnity. 'He's at your service, Ma'ams.'

One of the barkeeps unleashed a guffaw which was immediately quelled by Beecher's scorching glare.

Grace Clapp, head held high, had rolled back her cuffs, adopting a stance that implied she did this sort of thing every day. 'Lead him out,' she commanded. 'I'll do the measuring out here.'

Beecher shook his head. 'Oh no, Ma'am, far too dangerous when he's just been disturbed. He'd be sure to charge at us. The measuring will have to be done in the pen.'

Grace Clapp clucked her tongue, then assumed an expression of resolve.

'Very well,' she said. 'Open the gate.' She took the tape measure from her pocket.

Beecher drew back the bolt and did as instructed. 'Be careful he don't charge, Ma'am,' he said.

Grace Clapp stepped forward, the hem of her fine blue dress trailing in the slurry, her shoes immediately caked with muck. Peewee Poindexter followed her so closely, it appeared she was trying to hide in the larger woman's shadow.

It was now that a frightening thing happened. Porky stepped to the side so that he was hock deep in the large mud-puddle provided for his pleasure, unleashed a loud snort. With the stubs of his tusks thrust forward menacingly, he lowered his head.

Beecher again yelled a warning. '*My God, he's gonna charge!*'

At last Grace Clapp's fortitude drained away. She twisted in panicking retreat and in so doing collided with her diminutive companion. Amid shrieks of horror, both women fell into the slurry, splattering muck in all directions, coating themselves from bonnet to toe. Mrs. Clapp revealed an ample glimpse of her bloomer-style drawers, but

Peewee had sewn lead shot into the hem of her skirt to avoid embarrassment during every-day events such as falling arse over tit in a hog-pen.

Meanwhile, not to miss out on the fun, Porky had daintily bent his forelegs, lowered himself down and rolled onto his bristly back, working his shoulders from side to side. Splashing mud all around, he was snorting again, this time with sheer ecstasy, his stumpy legs threshing skywards.

Using Peewee like a cripple's crutch, Grace Clapp heaved her weight clumsily onto her feet, retreating from the pen, straightening her skirts and ignoring the shrieks of mirth that could no longer be subdued from the spectators — particularly from dark-haired Marie-Belle whose laugh resembled that of a jackass. Even Bent Nose Beecher was slapping his thighs in glee.

With a strange dignity, Peewee Poindexter also lifted herself from the mire, adjusting her boater. She stooped, retrieved the tape measure that had been dropped in the confusion. Showing unsuspected boldness, she plodded through the slurry, ignoring the shower that the pig was creating, unwound the measure and leaned over the beast. She whispered something into the pig's ear that was inaudible to spectators — something soothing, maybe loving. Perhaps it was even some sort of porcine bribe. Only she and Porky would ever know. But the animal lay on its back, perfectly still, seemingly smiling. Although it was never afterwards mentioned, it was almost as if Peewee took some pleasure in fondling his genitalia, murmuring soothingly, having found, it appeared, a sudden affection for the beast. Finally, she acquired the necessary reading — double-checked.

'Exactly eight inches,' she said as she emerged from the pen and fastened the gate behind her.

# 12

On the circus's second evening, Gregg Mason took the dark-haired Marie-Belle to see the show. They rode double on Gregg's sorrel horse, taking a circuitous route to Gilbey's Meadow so as to give them an opportunity for a little canoodling in the woods along the way. Afterwards, they left the sorrel tethered to a tree well to the rear of the great tent and proceeded on foot. Marie-Belle was a vivacious French mademoiselle, the younger sister of Violette La Plante. She was bubbling with excitement, her outrageous laugh working overtime. And when she wasn't laughing, she chatted away, skipping and flitting from subject to subject. On reaching the circus meadow, local womenfolk recognized her as one of Lucy May's soiled doves and contemptuously ignored her, whilst their men revealed no sign that they knew her bare bottom was as round and yielding as a ripe melon. No sign, apart from a slight reddening of the cheeks.

As for Gregg, he generally enjoyed the girl's company whether in bed or in secluded woods, and only recently had his enthusiasm to make a 'respectable woman' of her declined. As a matter of fact, ever since he'd met a certain Abigail Simmons in Fallow Springs.

Abigail was a highly respectable, young lady from a wealthy family. She had only recently returned to the family home, having been educated at an Eastern college. She was beautiful, all right, being tall and willowy, reminding you of a fine racehorse. On hearing Gregg claim he was marshal of Nelly's Nipple, she had shown immediate and amorous interest, totally ignorant of the fact that he had momentarily forgotten to mention the prefix 'deputy'. Still, as he'd told himself so often, Aaron couldn't go on forever. Not that he wished him any harm, for he was fond of the old boy.

Gregg's visits to Fallow Springs to comfort his ailing and elderly Aunt Claribel had become more frequent of late, despite the fact that Claribel had returned to remarkable health. Aaron had been generous in giving time-off to his deputy, expressing great sympathy for the aunt, and claiming that he also was in the 'ailing and elderly' category and might well be glad of a little sympathy himself shortly.

After Gregg and Marie-Belle had entered the packed big-top, they squeezed themselves onto a wooden plank seat. The tent was thick with baccy smoke, and the discordant brass band did not entirely drown out the hawking and spitting of the menfolk. Gregg had but a quarter-buttock perch at the very end of a row, but Marie-Belle was clinging on to him like a fresh-water leech. Their closeness enabled him to slap the hand of the man sitting on the other side of her, as it attempted to sneak up her thigh. Her tight grip reminded him that once he had told her that his life's ambition was to take her in holy matrimony and raise a houseful of little Marie-Belles. Since his acquaintance with Abigail, he knew that his ardor towards this soiled dove had cooled somewhat, but she seemed not to notice and he had no desire to upset her tonight.

Now, Alberto Cardoza, spectacularly garbed as Yankee Doodle Dandy, appeared, cracked his whip, and introduced his show as 'the greatest entertainment this side of the Golden Gate'. Amid applause, a hoard of clowns tumbled into the ring along with a mean-as-sin donkey that they attempted to climb aboard. Gregg wished that Marie-Belle would not laugh so loudly because the donkey glanced around with mounting interest, clearly imagining that the girl's braying laugh was a mating call.

There followed a succession of acts. The cow-girl Annie Hickock, in divided skirt, fringes and boots, demonstrated numerous shooting skills, extinguishing the flame of candle, massacring an apple at twenty feet shooting backwards from beneath her armpit, turning her back on a target and using a mirror to score a bull's-eye and finally inviting a fella from the audience to stand with a potato on his head which she indicated she would shoot off. She missed the first time, making a hole in his hat. Her second shot was even worse, for he was slammed back to the ground, an awful red stain spreading across his shirt-front.

Suddenly the place was in uproar; female members of the audience were screaming and menfolk were shaking their heads in dismay

'Oh . . . the poor devil's shot through the heart!' a woman behind Gregg cried out.

And Annie Hitchcock was shouting, 'Is there a doctor in the house!'

For a moment turmoil and confusion

reigned, then sanity was restored.

The seemingly dead individual jumped to his feet and, smiling broadly, spat a bullet out from his mouth, thereafter he bowed to the crowd, doffing his bullet-holed hat and indicating that the blood wasn't blood at all, but a ripe tomato that he'd held in his hand. He'd been planted in the audience, and now applause thundered.

Next came a display by Siberian roller skaters; then a man was fired into the air from a cannon, though you never actually saw him hurtling through the great puff of smoke. However, he, or somebody remarkably like him, immediately appeared hanging from the roof of the tent. After other acts that brought sighs of disbelief and applause from the audience — trick horse-riding, performing elephants, high-wire acrobats, jugglers — a high metal railing was erected in the ring to form a rotunda. Soon the musky smell of more animals added its pungency to the already thick atmosphere. Within the rotunda, a Canadian bear was attacked and subdued by a pack of huge dogs, who then repeated their success against a tired looking Opelousas bull.

But now the excitement was intensifying, for the climax of the show was approaching. Goliath the Lion, the amazing King of the Jungle, billed as the fiercest animal on God's earth, was due to fight a grizzly bear. The vanquished animal would then have fireworks and crackers attached to his back and career around the ring in terror as they exploded, all amid shrieks of guaranteed mirth from the audience. The entire act would be accompanied by the brass band giving a rendition of music by Tchaikovsky with real cannon fire.

As the previous act reached its conclusion and was cleared away, the audience waited with baited breath as drums rolled. But then a surprising thing happened. Alberto Cardoza appeared in the ring, his face full of dismay. Holding up his hand to quell the drums, he spoke in a voice laden with doom.

'Ladies and gentleman, I have an announcement of the gravest nature to make. We have been unable to restrain Goliath the Lion. He is a truly wild creature, and despite the valiant efforts of the Lion King, Georgio Skoff, who has been badly mauled and is indeed fortunate to survive, the lion has chewed through the bars of his cage and run off. Can I please ask for a round of applause for the gallant Georgio who has been struck down so savagely, and perhaps, tonight, you will pray that he will make a speedy recovery.'

He paused while a ripple of tentative clapping came from the audience, then he continued.

'I cannot emphasize sufficiently how deeply sorry I am that this magnificent animal is not present to perform this evening. We will certainly do our utmost to recover him at the earliest opportunity. Meanwhile I must warn you that as you proceed homeward after the show, you should stay in groups and keep your eyes peeled for danger. Goliath is extremely dangerous and could pounce at any time, so I beg you to be on your guard.'

The audience were now showing signs of unrest, even a booing from one section, but again Alberto Cardoza raised his arms and encouraged silence.

'All is not lost, my friends. We will not disappoint such a wonderful audience. Replacing the lion this evening, we have another sensational act. One that will leave you breathless with amazement. Ladies and gentlemen, I am truly proud to present William Brown who is just twelve years of age. He is indeed the most talented boy whistler ever, and will perform three of today's most popular songs. Please welcome the incredible William Br . . . '

The end of the announcement was drowned out by boos and jeers and the poor blond-headed boy never stood a chance of making himself heard, despite seeing this as his opportunity to step onto the world stage. Though he whistled manfully, he was totally drowned out by howls and hoots of dissatisfaction.

Later, the apprehensive crowd dispersed into the night, ever mindful that a ferocious beast was roaming through the darkness, and might, at this very moment, be watching for an easy victim to feed upon. Women clung to their men, and the whole situation engendered a craving among the female population for male protection — a craving that brought much bedded bliss in the subsequent hours and a possible rise in the birth rate nine months later.

Gregg and Marie-Belle left the tent and, in order to return to the tethered sorrel, left the main throng and walked through the mass of wagons, cages and circus impedimenta at the rear. Marie-Belle, as terrified of being attacked by the lion as every other female, stuck glue-like to Gregg's side. Above, the stars and moon were shining brightly.

They passed numerous circus folk who seemed too busy with their own activities to pay them any attention, but suddenly they came upon a cage on wheels. Its door hung open and beneath this, Gregg read the name-board — GOLIATH THE LION. He recalled that Cardoza had explained how the animal had chewed its way through the bars, but now, as he checked around, he could find no damage to the cage.

'What's zat noise!' Marie-Belle suddenly exclaimed, and they both froze in their tracks to listen.

A snarling, growling sound was clearly audible, threatening, close in, frightening.

# 13

'Ze lion!' Marie-Belle sobbed in fear.

Gregg shook his head, stooped down, peered beneath the cage. A smell of tornado juice probed into his nostrils, as thick on the air as vomit. Then the roar came again and he realized it was the sound of a man snoring. Investigating further, he struck a match for light and found a large fellow, dressed in a Roman toga, lying on his back in the shadow beneath the cage, a discovery now shared by Marie-Belle.

'Oo is it?' she enquired.

'I bet it's the Lion King,' Gregg responded. 'He's so pie-eyed he couldn't hit the ground with his hat. He don't seem a bit mauled, either.'

They backed out and, hand in hand, hurried on to where the patient sorrel was tethered. Gregg was thankful the horse had not been molested by the lion.

After they mounted up and she was pressing her breasts against his back, she murmured, 'Gregg, *chéri*, you said we might go for a picnic tomorrow. Zat would be really nice. I know you'd protect me from zat nasty lion.'

'Honey, I'm real sorry,' Gregg said, 'but I've promised to go to Fallow Springs tomorrow. My aunty's mighty sick.'

She sighed heavily, kicking her heels into the sorrel with frustration.

The next meeting of the Town Women's Guild & Temperance Society, called at short notice by Emily Grapewrath, was brief by necessity, for the air in the small upstairs room of the Methodist Church was impure. Some of the ladies held dainty handkerchiefs to their noses. This was despite a wide-open window and the fact that both Grace Clapp and Peewee Poindexter had changed their clothing and scrubbed their bodies nigh raw in a vain attempt to rid themselves of the stench of pig manure. Only the passage of time would restore their normal fragrance, and time was something Mrs. Grapewrath did not currently believe she had. Prompt action was necessary.

'Ladies,' she began with a sniff, 'first of all we all owe a debt of thanks to Grace and Peewee who undertook the unsavory task of measuring Mr. Beecher's pig. They proved themselves intrepid. They also proved beyond doubt that the representation of the pig on the mural is totally inaccurate, exceeding reality by no less than an entire quarter of an inch!'

A gasp of indignation followed by a ripple of applause went through the ladies at this apparent victory.

'I sent Mr. Beecher a note,' Emily Grapewrath continued, 'pointing out the true facts, but he has responded with an astounding claim and an almost unbelievable suggestion. The man is of the lowest character. If any of you are particularly sensitive, then all I can suggest is that you put your hands over your ears while I read Mr. Beecher's note.'

Around the table, the ladies looked at each other as if seeking courage and support. None placed their hands to their ears.

The minister's wife cleared her throat and read aloud in a steadfast voice.

'*Dear Ladies, it is a well-known fact that the size of the male member varies during times of stimulation and at certain times of the day. At the hour when the measuring ceremony took place, Porky's member was at its most quaggy, and therefore the findings were totally unfair. A pig's pecker is a bit like a corkscrew and sometimes it straightens out.*'

Emily Grapewrath paused, as if girding her loins for greater ordeal. She glanced around at the wide eyes of her listeners, then proceeded with Beecher's missive.

'*There maybe some ladies who will disagree when I say that such matters* are affected by the time of day. All I can do, with the utmost respect, is to refer them to their husbands when they first awake in the mornings and they will be obliged to agree with me.'

A wave of shock erupted around the table.

'Goodness me!' Esther Brown gasped.

Others could hardly believe their ears.

'I would ask,' Emily Grapewrath continued reading Beecher's words, 'that another measuring ceremony be arranged in the early morning when Porky's member will be larger, indeed in excess, I believe, of the depiction in the mural. Signed, Your humble servant, Bent Nose Beecher.'

Her voice trailed off into stunned silence.

The combination of the hot day and the overpowering porcine smell, topped by the shameless words written by Mr. Beecher, was too much for the delicate Cynthia Davis who normally recorded the minutes at such meetings but today had found it too distasteful. Looking deathly pale, her eyes took on a squint and she slid from her chair onto the floor, fainting away into the more ladylike realms of oblivion.

Emily ground her teeth wrathfully. *Beecher must pay for this.*

# 14

'Marshal McLean,' Alberto Cardoza said, wringing his fleshy hands in agitation, 'I have no alternative but to ask for your urgent help. *Most* urgent help.'

Aaron looked up from his desk and saw that the egg-shaped circus owner had stepped through the doorway. Aaron scooped the last few beans from a can and licked the spoon clean. He sensed trouble.

'What can I do for you, sir?'

'It's our lion, Goliath. He ran off last night and we haven't seen hide nor hair of him since. He's a real danger to the community, running wild, could pounce at any time when his belly starts to rumble.'

Aaron wiped his mouth with the back of his hand. He pondered on the circus owner's words.

'Surely, the lion king should find him, bring him back,' he remarked.

Cardoza shook his head, his eyes showing the glint of tears. 'Georgio is ill. You see, the lion mauled him when it escaped. He was lucky to survive, but he's very poorly, and we can't spare anybody else to go hunting because we have the rest of our shows to put on. Oh Marshal, I beg you to help us.'

Aaron eyed Cardoza suspiciously. 'You want me to go out and catch that beast?'

'Oh, Marshal, we'd be so grateful — and you could well be saving countless lives. Just imagine if that animal caught a child!'

Aaron fidgeted uneasily in his chair. 'I'm not trained to bring in lions. Findin' that lion could be harder than findin' a hoss-thief in Heaven. It's downright difficult enough to bring in criminals, but lions . . . '

'Everybody speaks so highly of you. Everybody says you've got real tracking skills. That if anybody can do it,

Marshal McLean, you're the man!'

'Flattery ain't gonna reap rewards,' Aaron said.

'But that lion's a great danger to the townsfolk of Nelly's Nipple, particularly the children and young women. Just imagine how bad you'd feel if there was some sort of tragedy!'

Aaron sighed, tapped his fingers three times on his desktop, then said, 'Guess I'll ride out this afternoon, see if I can find him.'

Cardoza was speechless with gratitude, the tears on his chubby cheeks shining. He would surely have kissed Aaron if the marshal had been that way inclined. He left, bowing and scraping and continuing to express his thanks as he climbed into his wagon and left town.

Mid-afternoon, Aaron saddled Mockey and persuaded her to carry him out to the circus grounds. He wished Gregg was with him, but he'd gone off to Fallow Springs to comfort his ailing aunt. Mockey was particularly ornery at having her siesta disturbed on this torrid afternoon, bucking and trying to nip him, but he kept the upper hand.

The usual exhibitions of balloons, wild animals and so on had attracted a crowd, but Aaron by-passed these, rode beyond the big-top, and entered the tangle of wagons, cages and general mess that represented the behind-the-scenes part of the show. He noticed Alberto Cardoza's caravan accommodation, much grander than any of the others; he ignored it, not hankering for any more of the man's greasy company.

He asked a fella washing down an elephant the way to the lion's cage and was directed to the far edge of the wagons where he found the cage marked GOLIATH.

The cage door stood open and a Mexican in a big sombrero was inside mucking it out. Aaron dismounted, feeling stiff after his ride. He inspected the exterior of the cage, reaching up to test the bars with his hands. Every thing seemed sturdy.

'Thought the lion chewed his way out of the cage,' he called to the Mexican working inside. 'Don't see no bite marks.'

The Mexican paused, leaned on his broom and pushed back his sombrero. Sweat was running down his swarthy face, turning his mustache into a soggy dish-mop. 'Repaired,' he explained.

Aaron pondered, then observed, 'Lion must be mighty strong, bitin' through iron.'

'*Si señor*,' the Mexican said. He seemed unable to string more than two words together at a time.

'Where's the lion-king?' Aaron asked. 'Gettin' ready for the bone yard?'

The Mexican shrugged, turned his mouth into an inverted horseshoe, and pointed his finger downward. Aaron followed his indication, peered between the wheels and was met by the familiar stench of rot-gut. The lion-king was sprawled beneath the cage, still clad in his toga. He immediately sat up, but he bumped his head on the underside of the cage and collapsed with a groan.

Aaron withdrew, waved his thanks to the Mexican, remounted the piebald and rode out onto the prairie backing the circus. He figured Goliath must have headed this way after he escaped. He wouldn't have paused to watch the show as he departed. Aaron wondered if the cage door, carelessly left wide open, might have encouraged the beast to seek his freedom. The whole business seemed downright fishy.

He spent an hour, cutting for sign, scouring the land north of the circus grounds, for a time figuring that the beast hadn't left enough tracks to trip an ant. But eventually he struck luck in the form of unmistakable lumps of lion-shit. God knew why Aaron considered it unmistakable. Maybe it was instinct. And soon after, in the mud along a river bank, he found the double tracks of paw-marks, the large width between the parallel lines indicating the passage of a large lion-sized creature. He glanced at the surrounding ridges, wondering if Goliath was spying on him, hugging the ground, ears pinned back as he prepared to charge. He'd once read that lions could catch you either by pouncing from a concealed place, or stalking and then running you down in a swift rush, biting you in the neck, disconnecting the spinal column. Aaron's spine began to itch and he took to looking back frequently. Furthermore, Mockey was chuntering to herself, curling her lip, rolling her eyes, pricking her ears. He could read her like a book and knew she was threatening to high-tail homeward at the slightest opportunity. Hilda had once chided him that he could understand horses as if they were his equals which, on reflection, she reckoned they were. He smiled to himself as his thoughts touched upon Hilda, then he realized he must save this pleasure for later, having other matters to attend to.

He consoled himself with the knowledge that both dung and tracks were cold trail. Goliath could be miles away by now.

The land about him, spotted with flowers of every color, undulated with dips and swells, making long-distance viewing difficult, but he heeled the piebald along the river-bank and presently discovered more lion tracks where Goliath had turned away from the water. Thereafter, he found an area where the grass was flattened, indicating that the beast had taken a breather. Further tracks beckoned him onward, mile upon mile, and presently a new concern plagued him. He was heading straight onto *Golden Rooster* land, the domain of Lyle Cameron and his hoodlum cowpokes. And if Cameron became aware of his presence, things could turn ugly — but he was determined to follow the trail. Cardoza had been right. Such a fierce animal prowling the country would be a menace to any folks crossing his path, and no grazing cow would be safe.

Thunder was rumbling in the heavens, indicating that a summer storm wasn't far away, and the wind was rustling the prairie grass, causing it to move and sway as if something was moving through it. A meadowlark was sounding off, close at hand, subduing her cry to almost a whisper. The air had taken on a coolness so Aaron put on his yellow slicker, disregarding the fact that such a bright color might attract attention.

Presently he stopped, or rather Mockey stopped; no amount of heel thumping would drive her forward when she figured it was time for a rest, so Aaron gave his backside a respite, and allowed his saddle to cool while he rolled himself a smoke. He also ate some of the pork sandwiches that Lucy May had insisted he brought. He was on a considerable hillock, and way off in the distance he could see the great archway that Cameron had erected to indicate the start of *Golden Rooster* land. He was looking at it from the inside, which didn't bring him any comfort. He gazed around at the undulating terrain, seeing the brown-and-white speckling of grazing Herefords, seemingly unconcerned that a predator, one of Nature's most formidable and efficient killers, was on the prowl. Aaron strained his eyes to see the beast, but to no avail. Thankfully, nor could he spot any of Cameron's cowboys.

When he pushed on, large spots of rain had started to fall, the clouds had swung in, making the sky look like a sheet of gray tarpaulin, across which a black arrowhead of geese aimed north-ward. The tracks he discovered, sparse as they were, were leading him deeper and deeper into the heart of the *Golden Rooster* empire.

# 15

It was strange how, when he'd been trying his hardest to find something, it nearly scared the pants off him when he stumbled across it. All because he had allowed his thoughts to swing to other matters, like how he'd eventually have to ride into Lyle Cameron's ranch house and drag Billy out at the point of a gun, that is if he could find him. Of course the boy could have fled the territory, but he had the feeling that Billy was too yellow-bellied to step away from his pa's protection. And there was that damned pig! What the hell could a simple, nigh law-abiding lawman do to restore harmony between the community's female and male sexes? All he'd ever wanted was a peaceful life. This sort of trouble had never been dreamed of when he'd first pinned on a marshal's badge. If he'd had a crystal ball, he'd have refused it there and then.

*But there he was* — Goliath, his sandy back turned, black-tufted tail twitching. He was gazing into the distance, no doubt seeking sight of his next meal and flexing his claws at the thought. Or maybe he was looking for female company, anxious to start his own pride and not realizing that the nearest available lioness was most likely on the other side of the Atlantic.

Mockey was as surprised as the man on her back, her normal demeanor rising to new meanness as her nostrils flared to the scent of lion and she reared, unleashing a whinny fit to raise the dead.

The lion twisted around. His lips drew back, snarl-like, his large eyes pools of amber. The animal looked far bigger from the front than from the back, far more majestic and self assured. The sight had gooseflesh prickling all over Aaron. The beast's jaws hung slightly open, revealing the big yellow canines, ideal shearing tools for tearing at tendons and fleshy bones.

Aaron flattened himself along the piebald's back, clinging on for dear life, his gaze none the less locked with the lion's unflinching stare, believing that he might charge at any moment. Somehow, Aaron calmed the troublesome nag and grabbed for his gun, ignoring the pain in his rheumatic fingers as he clawed the weapon from its leather.

He realized that he might have to shoot Goliath.

But now he became aware that Mockey was performing one of her favorite tricks: walking backwards so sneakily that you didn't realize you were moving until you noticed everything in front growing smaller. Mockey didn't take to lions, there was no denying. As a temporary concession, Aaron allowed the nag to have her way, eventually turning her, at the same time thanking the Lord that the lion hadn't charged. When they had vacated the immediate scene, he reined in, smoothed the piebald's neck and whispered some soothing words into her ear: 'Play me up anymore, and I'll kick hell out o' you, you damned fleabit nag!'

Gentled, she submitted to being tethered to a cottonwood tree. Having holstered his gun, he went to his saddlebags and removed the leftovers of the sandwiches Lucy May had provided, anticipating that some bribery might be necessary if the lion was hungry. He then removed his grass and fiber throw-rope from his saddle horn. It had turned kind of green from lack of use. He'd made it himself many years since. Initially, it had been rough and prickly and he'd burned it with paper to get rid of the loose fibers; now it seemed pretty smooth, though stiff with age like he was.

He paused, wondering if he was acting prudently. It occurred to him that if the lion killed him, the piebald would be at the lion's mercy, being tethered. On the other hand, if he left the horse unsecured, she'd hightail off in next to no time. He debated the issue. He decided he'd better not leave the piebald disadvantaged. Unfastening Mockey, he appealed to her sense of fairness. 'You stay here until I get back. If I don't get back, hightail it quick.'

He reckoned the ornery beast understood his words, for she nodded her head and blew down her nose, making a noise like an old man's fart. Hilda would have sworn the horse comprehended the situation, being of equal status to Aaron.

So he left her unfastened, and armed with throw-rope, sandwiches and his pistol, he returned to the lion. Goliath was licking his paw, as if all the walking had left him lame. He looked up as Aaron approached and positioned himself some five yards distant.

The marshal uncoiled his rope, adjusting the metal slip-honda so's the noose would drop over a lion's head, shaggy mane included. He'd have to be careful. The honda could knock out a horse's eye if thrown inaccurately — or a lion's, which would make Goliath mighty angry. It had been a long time since he'd done any rope work, but he figured he hadn't lost the skill entirely. The only trouble was that his arms were so downright painful and stiff from the rheumatics.

The lion had stood up, looking at him as if he was crazy, but Aaron ignored thoughts of the animal's inner opinions. He whirled the rope about his head and made his first throw, groaning with the hurt it caused him. The noose fell a good two feet wide of target. He recovered the rope and enlarged the noose. His second throw was no more successful. But he recalled the saying 'third time lucky' and this was almost true, for the third throw actually struck the lion's great face, made him blink, before dropping to the ground.

Aaron cursed, rubbed his throwing arm.

Goliath made no move, apart from licking his black lips.

Aaron said, 'Dammit!' He had to admit it: his loop just wasn't hungry enough. So, taking a great risk, he paced up to the beast and, using both hands, placed the noose squarely over Goliath's head and pulled it tight. As he did so, Goliath took two steps forward, behaving like a dog on a lead. Aaron offered his left-over sandwich to the lion who took a sniff but declined, turning away as if to say he preferred antelope in his sandwiches.

To Aaron's astonishment, the beast followed him, without even a tug on the rope, as he returned to the spot where he'd left Mockey. As expected, the horse had run off, was probably by now burning up the trail towards Nelly's Nipple.

Aaron shivered. The rain was pelting down, a cold wind was getting up and the light was fading fast. Furthermore, he was tired and he guessed that Goliath felt the same way. None the less, he figured he'd better cover a few miles before he took a rest, that was if

Goliath agreed — which he did. He'd never known such a placid lion, in fact, apart from the odd mountain lion, he'd never known any lions at all, though he'd always imagined they could be downright ornery if aroused. He determined not to arouse Goliath who followed along quite willingly as he started on the long walk homeward. Aaron considered riding on the lion's back but discarded the idea. Nobody would believe his story when he got back, and anyway it would look damned stupid; a town marshal traveling astride a lion!

After an hour of plodded amity, the rainy night had blackened and the two considered it was time to rest. Aaron tethered the lion to a sturdy oak tree, growing amid a thicket, and searched around for a suitable place for himself, eventually finding a spot where the grass grew thick. He wished the thoughtless Mockey hadn't galloped off with his tarp-wrapped bedroll, but that was typical of her. She never considered anybody but her damned self.

He was about to bed down for the night, when, on second thoughts, he rose and returned to where the lion had settled, figuring a double knot in the rope might be more prudent. Goliath, who was lying down by now, watched him with questioning eyes as he undertook the task but made no comment, not even a whimper. Aaron patted the animal's head, then returned to his own spot. He'd once read a story about a slave called Androcles and how he'd removed a thorn from a lion's swollen paw during biblical times, thereafter being the animal's pal for life. Now he figured he was somewhat of an Androcles himself. And as for that fella Daniel entering the lions' den. Well, if them critters were as pussy-friendly as Goliath, it was no great deal. Aaron was glad he hadn't been obliged to shoot Goliath for it would have been a grave injustice, seeing as that he was so uncomplaining. No doubt circus train-ing had quelled the wild and savage instincts in him, apart from when he was required to put on an act for the show.

Aaron settled down in the grass, his fingers laced behind his head, using his back as a mattress and his belly for covering. He could hear the rain pelting against the leaves above his head. He felt uncomfortable and knew the dampness would seep in his bones, making his rheumatism twice as bad come morning. But he was tuckered and after ten minutes he was snoring blissfully.

Just after dawn poked up, he had a nasty shock.

# 16

Aaron came awake. He tried to roll off his bunk, then attempted to lower his feet, but they wouldn't lower. He was on the ground already, under a tree.

A boot in the ribs had disturbed him. He blinked the sleep from his eyes, found himself looking up into the ugly split-lip face of Will Brosker, the usual red bandanna around his throat.

'Didn't figure my eyes was deceivin' me,' Brosker announced. 'If it ain't my ole pal, Marshal McLean.' He had drawn his pistol, thumbed back the hammer, had the weapon aimed at Aaron's head. 'You must be plum loco, comin' back to these parts. I been swearin' blind that I'd get even with you for what you did the other day. I suppose you're spyin' out to catch young Billy. You won't get him though. His daddy won't let you! Anyway, you won't be in no condition to chase anybody after I finished with you.'

Aaron groaned, forcing himself up into sitting position. He completed his usual morning ablutions by wiping his hands over his face.

'What actual condition am I gonna be in, when you've finished with me? You gonna cut me up into little bits and feed me to the buzzards?'

Brosker snarled real mean, waving his pistol. 'Don't treat this as a joke, old man. First thing I'll do is finish the job I started the other day. I'll shoot that damned nag o' yours.'

Aaron made a scoffing sound. 'You'll have a job. She ain't keepin' company with me right now. She ran off in a tizzy.'

Brosker blustered for a moment and Aaron noticed how red his cheeks were. It was like he was suffering from high blood pressure. 'Stand up, old man. I don't like killin' folks when they're sittin' down.'

Aaron grunted with displeasure. 'And

I don't like bein' hassled first thing in the mornin'.' With great effort, he hoisted his stiff body into standing position.

'An' don't think you'll die quick,' Brosker said. 'It'll be slow and painful, like you dawgone deserve.'

'I ain't never been threatened like that,' Aaron commented, 'not since Hilda left me.'

Brosker hadn't finished. 'You'll have more holes in you than a cabbage after a hailstorm.'

'Exactly how you gonna fix that?' Aaron enquired, cocking his head, as calm as if they were discussing chicken feed.

It was then a stepped-on twig cracked behind Brosker. His split-lipped mouth sagged and he twisted round — then jumped a good foot off the ground with shock.

Goliath, had moved out from the thicket, standing with the chewed-through rope dangling from his neck. His great, raspy tongue rolled around his lips, indicating it was time for breakfast. Aaron knew that bulls got mighty angry at the sight of a red rag. Could it be that Brosker's red bandanna might have a similar effect on a lion? But Goliath gazed at Brosker in a manner of complete docility, no doubt wondering what the hell all the fuss was about.

The legs of the cowpuncher seemed to have turned to rubber. The pistol had dropped from his fingers. He was clutching his chest, his breathing coming in quick-fire gasps. He completed what a dancer would call a pirouette and then sagged to the ground in an untidy heap.

'*Goddammit!*' he choked. '*W-what's that!*'

'That's a lion,' Aaron explained, 'fiercest creature on the planet. King of all beasts.'

Aaron figured it was time for his first smoke of the day. He reached into his pocket and fumbled with the makings, concluding that Brosker was like a hard boiled egg; all yellow inside.

'Keep him off me, for God's sake.' Brosker was struggling for his words. 'Shouldn't . . . shouldn't be allowed, scarin' the livin' daylights outa innocent folk.'

'Down boy,' Aaron said to Goliath who looked decidedly dozy, almost as if he was considering going back to bed, there being nothing of greater interest taking place.

Aaron lit his smoke, took a deep, calming draw. Brosker seemed mighty poorly. His face had changed from red to blue and he was still snatching at his breath as if each time might be his last.

'I n-need a doc real bad,' he groaned. He was affected by all-over shuddering. 'It's my damned ticker. Always been a problem.'

Aaron chewed that over. Didn't seem right to let the fella suffer. Maybe he should put him out of his misery with a bullet in the head, like a horse with a broken leg. But no, that wouldn't be Christian.

'You gotta a horse somewhere?' he asked, taking another draw from his smoke.

Brosker was crumpled on the ground, doubled over with pain. He nodded, made a gesture with his hand. 'Hundred yards . . . in the trees.'

'I'll go fetch him,' Aaron said.

'D-don't leave me with this monster!' Brosker pleaded, his fear-burning eyes settling on Goliath.

'He'll be all right,' Aaron reassured him. 'I'll offer him what's left of my sandwich. Mebbe his appetite's improved since yesterday. He'll stand guard while I'm gone.'

This time Goliath ate the sandwich quite appreciatively, licking his lips and using his claw as a tooth-pick after he'd finished.

Aaron found the bay horse, tethered where Brosker had indicated. The animal was still saddled and highly agitated because he could smell lion on the air. But with his usual expertise, Aaron gentled him and returned to where Brosker was sprawled.

One thing was certain. The cowboy wasn't going to pose any more threats for some time. It might well be that he would cash in his chips before they could get to the doc at Nelly's Nipple.

# 17

The journey was not the easiest. Aaron rode the bay horse with Brosker, continually groaning, mounted up behind him, clinging real hard and going into sort of spasms at irregular intervals. The bay horse wasn't in the mood for lingering. What horse would be with a lion padding along on his heels?

When they eventually reached the circus grounds at Gilbey's Meadow, Goliath seemed pleased to be home and jumped into his cage without the need for goading. Aaron was quite sad to leave him as he'd grown to enjoy the animal's company, but he determined not to get too sentimental over it. Cardoza of course was oozing with gratitude, pumping Aaron's hand over and over, and inviting him to eat some home-reared circus food, but Aaron declined, having no wish to have a performing animal on his plate.

Brosker was so ill, he was practically falling off the horse, and Cardoza offered to convey the patient to Nelly's Nipple in a wagon. Aaron accepted the offer, thinking that maybe the circus owner wasn't all that bad.

Brosker was assisted to a wagon and driven off by one of the circus underlings. Aaron breathed a sigh of relief, figuring he had done his duty. He was standing close to Cardoza's grand accommodation, starting to remount the bay horse, having borrowed him on temporary basis from Brosker, when a familiar scent wafted to his nostrils. Mixed in with all the animal smells that tainted the air, he was unable to identify it — but sure enough he'd smelt it before. He figured it might be the perfume that Hilda used to rub behind her ears.

*Hilda* . . . she kept returning to his mind, more with each year that passed. He pined for her nagging tongue and tiresome ways real bad — but life had to go on.

He set out on his way back to town, feeling kinda proud. It was quite something to recover an escaped lion, quite educational. Mind you, he'd missed his cell-bunk last night. It'd been a good many years since he'd last slept beneath the stars, and his bones were still aching from it.

He was just a half-mile from Nelly's Nipple when he saw a rider approaching, the gait of his horse familiar. It was Gregg Mason and he was moving from side to side, as if he was searching the ground for sign, which subsequently proved to be the case. Looking up, he gave Aaron a wave and a few minutes later they met up and reined in their mounts.

'If you're lookin' for that lion, you're too late,' Aaron said. 'I brought him in.'

'Ain't lion-sign I'm huntin' for,' Gregg volunteered. 'It's pig-sign.'

'Pig-sign?'

'Sure, Porky's gawn missin'. When

Beecher took him his breakfast this mornin', he'd disappeared.'

'Well I be danged!' Aaron said. 'Thought we had a guard posted?'

Gregg shook his head. 'Arnie Closcher took sick last night, had to go home. You wouldn't think so to see him now, though. He's been drinkin' real heavy in *Porky's Pride* all day.'

'Mebbe he was bribed,' Aaron said. 'Mebbe them women have got at him.'

'Could be,' Gregg nodded, 'but a lot o' folks figure the lion got him. Eaten him up lock stock and barrel.'

Aaron scratched his jaw thoughtfully. 'Come to think of it, Goliath didn't want them sandwiches I offered him yesterday. Mebbe he was full up.'

'Them big-bug ladies are sure celebratin',' Gregg said. 'No matter what's happened to Porky.' He paused, then recalled something. 'There's another thing I better tell you. Lucy May's real anxious to see you.'

'She's desperate for my body, I suppose.'

'No. It ain't that, Aaron. It's somethin' more important. I don't know what. She seemed mighty stirred up, wouldn't tell me what was on her mind.'

Aaron nudged the bay horse forward. 'You carry on searchin' for that pig. He may turn up yet. I'll see you when you get back.'

Gregg waved his hand. Aaron rode at a good hickory back to Nelly's Nipple, wondering what was eating at Lucy May. Maybe she knew something about Porky.

# 18

'Aaron, Billy Cameron's got the real hots on one of my girls, Lily. I found out he's been making regular visits, sneaking into town every Thursday at midnight and going up to her room via the back way of the saloon.'

Aaron was all ears. He and Lucy May were sitting at a table in the far corner of the saloon. In the background, a man was tinkling on the ivories. There weren't many customers, but Lucy May kept her voice down, checking every so often that nobody was listening.

Aaron had set her up with champagne and she sipped at it appreciatively. He was making do with a glass of milk.

He said, 'Can't help feelin' it would be sinful, catchin' Billy with his pants down.'

'All those prissy women,' she said,

'would reckon what Billy was up to was sinful anyway. That, on top of killing Silas Fogwell. He deserves to be caught.'

'That maybe true, but it wouldn't do your trade any good. When the news leaked out that he'd been arrested while samplin' nookie. Some fellas with guilty consciences might reckon it was unprofessional and would be put off payin' visits.'

Lucy May laughed. 'Take more than that to staunch men's hungry desires. And my girls need have nothing to do with it. Gregg could slip the Mickey Fin into Billy's whiskey, and Lily would carry on as usual until Billy dozed off on her.' She laughed again. 'Probably take it as an insult. But then you and Gregg would arrive to carry Billy off to the jail.'

Aaron pondered on the suggestion. It was outrageous, but it appealed to him.

He nodded.

She rested her slim hand on his arm affectionately. 'I'll arrange it as a special favor to you, Aaron. I know how bad you want to catch that boy.'

He finished his milk. She leaned across and smoothed the cream from his cookie-duster with her finger. He then licked her finger clean.

Suddenly he said, 'Pig shit!'

'Pardon me!' Lucy May responded.

'It was pig shit I smelt when I was at the circus today. Didn't recognize it at the time.'

'Pig shit?' she said, still puzzled.

'Yup, pig shit, sure as Texas. I reckon that lion didn't gobble up Porky at all. Maybe that pig's been kidnapped.'

Lucy May nodded thoughtfully. 'Could be. Beecher told me that Alberto Cardoza made him an offer for the pig, said it would be wonderful for his show, but Beecher turned him down. Said all the tea in China wouldn't be enough for Porky. Cardoza went off in a right temper.'

'And the fella on guard, Arnie Closcher, has been wearin' calluses on his elbows, leaning on the bar ever since, like he's come into an inherit-ance.'

'Maybe he was bribed to be sick,' Lucy May commented, reinforcing Aaron's opinion.

★ ★ ★

The circus only had two more days to run. Business had been good because many of the folks who'd been there on the night the lion escaped, went back to see the show again, now that he was restored. After discussing matters, both Aaron and Gregg figured that despite the ill feeling of the town's big bug women, they were not wicked enough to contrive evil skullduggery. The most straight forward explanation for Porky's disappearance was that he had been kidnapped by the circus folk. The whole business of the lion's escape had puzzled Aaron, seeing that the bars hadn't been chewed, nor showed any signs of the repair that the Mexican mucker-out had claimed.

'Could be the whole thing was fixed,' Gregg suggested. 'Cardoza let the lion escape, knowin' they could catch it any time they chose. Their idea was to get you away from town while they rustled the pig. Cardoza's been hankerin' for that pig. He most likely heard about it before he got here.'

Aaron scratched his jaw. He figured Gregg was right.

Accordingly, in the small hours of the following night, the two lawmen, with considerable dedication to duty, deserted their beds and saddled their horses. Shortly, they were leaving town, riding out under a bright moon towards Gilbey's Meadow. As they drew close, the unmistakable smell of animals wafted to them. Despite raising his nose and sniffing real hard, Aaron couldn't discern any scents peculiar to Porky.

As they passed through a copse, Aaron said, 'Figure we'll leave our hosses here and go in on foot.'

Gregg nodded and they dismounted and tethered their animals. Aaron

149

didn't fancy walking back to Nelly's Nipple, nor riding double, so he made certain Mockey was fixed doubly secure. The two men then proceeded across the meadow towards the shadowy outlines of the big-top and the adjacent wagons, hoping that all the circus folk and their dogs were tucked up in bed.

'If that pig's anywhere,' Aaron whispered, 'he'll be near Cardoza's wagon.'

Soon they had cat-footed their way around the tent and were passing various cages from which the snores of sleeping animals could be heard. Next, they went close to the better class accommodation wagons, all unlit. Aaron figured these must belong to the artistes. From one came the sounds of heavy breathing and mounting sighs of satisfaction that indicated some private performance was being enacted. Aaron wondered what it was like to have nookie with an acrobat. Pretty demanding, he thought. He figured he would be too old for that sort of thing himself.

'Up ahead, on the left,' he whispered in Gregg's ear, pointing to Cardoza's great wagon. Alongside stood another smaller wagon. It had a curved, metal top and wooden sides. Some steps led up to its closed door.

Both lawmen froze as they glimpsed the glimmer of a cigarette. It was immediately snubbed out, but it was clear somebody was standing in the shadows of the metal-topped wagon, maybe a guard.

Aaron whispered he would deal with the matter, and leaving Gregg hidden in the gloom, he crept forward, hoping that his creaking joints wouldn't give him away. He took a circular route, coming around at the rear of the wagon. He was a shadow's breadth behind the guard as the latter fumbled with his matches to spark off a light for his next smoke. He couldn't seem to get his match to flare, and Aaron reached into a pocket for his own match and immediately offered his services.

'I got a light here.'

151

'*Santa Maria!*'

The man nigh jumped out of his skin, dropping cigarette and matches.

It was the Mexican Aaron had met when inspecting Goliath's cage.

'I got a light,' Aaron repeated, stooping to pick up the smoke the Mexican had dropped. He passed this back to him. The Mexican appeared to be struck dumb, never having been over-talkative anyway. Right now, the whites of his eyes showed like reclining new-moons.

Aaron struck a light and the Mexican, trembling, replaced the cigarette between his lips and accepted the flame.

Aaron was now quite sure that the pig was in the adjacent wagon. There was no mistaking the porcine stench for Hilda's perfume this time, it being in closer proximity.

'I come to take the pig back,' he said.

The Mexican found his tongue. 'No, señor. Cardoza want keep it.'

'Never mind about Cardoza. It's a serious matter, pig theft. You wouldn't want to be arrested as an accomplice, would you?'

'No, *señor*.' The man was puffing overtime on his smoke, as if it might be his last. 'I do nothin' wrong!'

Gregg had loomed from the shadows and his large and additional presence increased the Mexican's nervousness.

'Open up the wagon, Gregg,' Aaron instructed.

The deputy mounted the steps and drew back the iron bolt on the wagon's door, swung it open. As if well aware of developing events, Porky appeared, his moist snout catching a glint of moonlight as he half fell down the steps and stood with his customary enquiring expression.

'Yeah, watcha want?'

But suddenly a new voice lashed at them.

'Stay where you are, *señors*, or I'll shoot you.'

Cardoza, clad in silk dressing gown, had appeared from his wagon, a rifle in his hands.

# 19

'Now hold on, Alberto,' Aaron said.
'We're just recoverin' stolen property.
Ain't no crime in that.'

'The pig isn't stolen property,'
Cardoza snarled. 'I don't know what
you're talking about.'

'Hold fast. That pig's Porky. You
know it. I know it. And you lured me
outa town and bribed Arnie Closcher
so you could steal him. Now let's talk
turkey.'

Aaron felt annoyed at Cardoza's
stupid arguing. He did something he
didn't normally favor, kicking helpless
beasts, unless it was his horse Mockey
acting mean. He drew back his leg and
rammed his boot squarely against
Porky's unsuspecting backside. The
animal unleashed an outraged squeal
and took off like a thunderbolt. Beecher
had claimed that Porky could run real

154

fast and now he was proved right, though the beast blundered into several obstructions.

'Damn you!' Cardoza snarled. 'You've asked for this!'

He was raising his gun to vent his fury, but seemed to have some trouble in working the mechanism.

Aaron spoke, replacing his normal slow drawl with words of urgency. In so doing he lied through his teeth, or rather through his dentureless gums.

'My best buddy is the rancher Lyle Cameron. He's got an army of hoodlum cowpunchers, all of who love that pig real bad. Furthermore, they know where he is and unless he's back at the saloon by tomorrow, they'll ride in here and wreck your circus . . . and let all these poor animals out of their stinkin' cages!'

'No!' Cardoza cried out.

'Yes!' Aaron countered. 'Now put down that gun, otherwise those cowpunchers'll ride in here anyway. They're just mad to bust your show up.

I'll do my best to restrain them, but I can't promise much.'

Cardoza cursed in Spanish. It wasn't pleasant on the ear. He lowered the gun, the pique took hold of him and he hurled the weapon to the ground. Lucky it didn't go off.

'One more thing,' Aaron went on. 'I'm arrestin' you on a charge of pig theft. I'm takin' you in to stand trial.'

'You can't do that,' Cardoza exclaimed. 'The show's moving on day after tomorrow.'

'Well, you won't be with it,' Aaron said. 'I guess they'll manage without you. Probably a damn sight better. Seems to me, you ain't the most popular o' bosses.'

Gregg had stepped in close to Cardoza, his pistol drawn.

'Now unless you come along without further argument,' Aaron went on, 'we'll get those cowpunchers to wreck the show, and that's a promise.'

Fury pulsed through Cardoza's egg shaped body. If he'd had a spout in the top of his head steam would have been gushing out — but suddenly all the strength seemed to leave him and he looked like what he was: a deflated Humpty Dumpty.

'No judge'll be able to pin anything on me,' he mumbled.

A few minutes later, when Aaron and Gregg left the circus grounds, a sullen Alberto Cardoza went with them, his hands bound behind his back.

On arrival in town, the circus owner was consigned to the jail, Aaron resenting that he had to give up his sleeping place. Next morning Bent Nose Beecher was informed that if he wanted his pig back, he'd better go out and find him — no doubt the animal was foraging somewhere near Gilbey's Meadow. The saloon owner gratefully accepted the advice, took a couple of barkeeps with him and set out. By that afternoon Porky was reinstalled at the saloon, though he had a problem sitting down for a day or two, showing a distinct bruise alongside his curly tail, and his manner towards Aaron was decidedly off hand. The marshal felt quite guilty, having kicked the pig so hard, but at the time it had seemed the best way of resolving the situation.

Aaron next telegraphed Circuit-riding Judge, Isaac C. Marrow. With luck, there might shortly be more than one customer for judicial attention.

★   ★   ★

Next day being Thursday, Gregg left for his weekly visit to Fallow Springs, promising he'd be back before nightfall. This was the night Aaron intended to spring his trap, as suggested by Lucy May, and provide company in the cell for Alberto Cardoza. Company in the form of Billy Cameron. Cardoza spent the whole morning cursing those 'sonsofbitches' at the circus for not showing any concern over his incarceration; they didn't even bring him a fresh set of clothes. In consequence he cut a ludicrous figure behind bars, squatting on the wooden bunk in his sophisticated red-silk dressing gown.

To Aaron's surprise, Gregg returned early from Fallow Springs, on the mid-afternoon stage. He looked real flushed, and complained that he'd had a blazing row with his aunt and that she'd told him to take a running jump. In truth, he'd discovered that Abigail Simmons was two-timing him, having taken up with a classy young man who was the son of a senator. In comparison, she now realized that Gregg was downright common, and he had taken advantage of her generous and sensual nature. Of course Gregg didn't mention this to Aaron, leaving the old man to ponder on how devious and ungrateful elderly female relatives could be.

Meanwhile, Gregg had decided to rekindle his affections towards Marie-Belle, figuring he could live with her laugh after all.

But that night, there was no time for social pleasures. Aaron prayed that Billy Cameron hadn't lost his red-hot lust for

Lily and would creep into town at the darkest hour for nookie, little suspecting what was lined up for him.

With Lucy May's assistance, Gregg spent the evening mixing up the concoction intended to send Billy into the deepest slumber, mixing it with whiskey and sipping it himself to test it. It worked. Lucy May and Aaron spent a whole ten minutes dragging him back from his dream-world, fearing that he'd be too drowsy to undertake his duties that night. Fortunately, he eventually swam back to full consciousness, but in so doing spoke of some female named Abigail in the most disrespectful terms.

'Is his aunt called Abigail?' Lucy May asked.

'Claribel,' Aaron said, 'like a cow.'

Lucy May laughed. 'Abigail sounds like a cow too, according to Gregg.'

# 20

That night, Aaron turned off his lamp while *Porky's Pride* was still emitting sounds of its customary revelry from down the street. He figured it would be best to give the impression he and Gregg were retiring early. By eleven, the saloon had thrown out its last drunkard and in the marshal's office silence would have reigned had it not been for Cardoza's thunderous snoring coming from the cell. Aaron, as he slumped in his chair, reckoned it would be best if he kept awake and watchful, and the racket coming from behind the bars assisted him in this matter. Gregg had settled on the floor in the corner, his back against the wall, his hat over his eyes.

About half an hour after midnight, Marie Belle came tip-toeing across the street and her breathless, French voice imparted the news that Billy Cameron had arrived and was currently being entertained by Lily, who was unaware that his whiskey had been spiked. Marie Belle suggested that Aaron and Gregg should present themselves at Lily's room in fifteen minutes to collect Billy who, ''opefully, will be away wiz ze fairies by zen.'

As Marie Belle gave Gregg a quick kiss and scurried away, the two lawmen prepared themselves for the task ahead, strapping on their shooting irons. At the appointed time, they crossed the street, staying clear of creaking boardwalks, and crept down the alley at the side of the saloon. They noticed how a faint light showed through a curtained window, and Gregg whispered that this was Lily's room. Steep wooden steps led up the outside wall to the upper floor, and the young deputy was well ahead of Aaron, whose stiff legs slowed him in mounting most anything — apart from Lucy May.

So Gregg reached the top floor first,

entered through an open doorway and moved stealthily along the interior corridor. He was well aware that Lily's 'entertaining' room was next to Marie-Belle's and he saw a crack of light showing beneath the door. He took a deep breath, drew his pistol, and turned the door handle. It was locked. Stepping back, he pushed his entire weight against the door, splintering it inwards and stumbling through.

A surprising sight was revealed.

Lily was lying on the bed, naked as a jaybird, her pale, beautiful body reminiscent of a Pre-Raphaelite painting that had recently appeared in a gentleman's magazine. Her eyes were closed, the rise and fall of her pink-buttoned breasts and the smile on her lips indicating that her dreams were sweet.

Gregg reluctantly tore his eyes from her. He noticed how the window was open and the curtains, caught by the breeze, billowed inwards. Suddenly, there was the sound of a scuffle from under the window, and Aaron's voice cried, 'Take one step, Billy Cameron, an' I'll shoot you same way as you shot Silas Fogwell!'

The only retort was a scorching, blasphemous curse from Billy.

When Gregg looked from the window, he saw Billy stooped over. He was rubbing his leg. He'd obviously injured himself when jumping, it being quite a drop from the window. But no doubt he was hurt even more by the fact that Aaron, still half way up the outside stairs, had his gun trained on him.

'Unbuckle your gunbelt, Billy!' Aaron snapped.

'Can't,' the youngster retorted. 'It's holdin' my pants up.'

Aaron showed a rare compassion. 'Well, raise your hands then.'

A moment later the two lawmen were bundling the cursing youngster to the jail. Somehow suspecting trickery was afoot, Billy had thought himself pretty smart in swapping his drink with Lily's, but it had done him no good.

Cardoza was as tetchy as a teased snake at having to share his space, complaining his privacy was being violated. Aaron ignored him. There was only one bunk in the cell, and as the two inmates attempted to settle for the night, it became evident that the bunk was only wide enough to afford support for Billy's legs, shoulders and head. The egg-shaped bulge of the circus owner's middle compelled Billy's backside to overlap the side. Striving to preserve the peace, Aaron supplied Billy with a blanket to spread upon the floor, after which Gregg double-checked the cell door to make sure it was secure.

Next morning Doctor Henry Clapp examined Billy's shin, figuring it might be broken. He applied a splint and bound the ungrateful youngster's legs together with thick bandage, advising a week's cell-rest.

'Can't have a fella limping his way to the gallows,' he said.

# 21

Conscious that Aaron was feeling weary due to recent stresses, and also that he only had his office chair to sleep in, the cell-bunk being currently unavailable, Lucy May kindly offered him a share in her own bed the following night. Gratefully accepting, Aaron left Gregg guarding the prisoners.

Circuit Judge Isaac C. Marrow had responded to the request for his services, telegraphing back to say that he would arrive in Nelly's Nipple on Wednesday of the following week and reserving accommodation at the local hotel.

After *Porky's Pride* had ejected its late-night clients, Gregg was sitting in Aaron's chair, listening to the unmelodic snoring of the prisoners and still smarting at the way he'd been two-timed by Abigail Simmons, when a voice coming from the street startled him.

'Marshal, we come to take Billy home. Let him out an' there'll be no trouble.'

Gregg straightened in his chair, cursing to himself. Sure enough he recognized the voice of Seth Cranshaw, one of Cameron's hoodlums. And as he stepped into the doorway of the office, he saw that Cranshaw was accompanied by three more cowpunchers, appearing as shadows in the moonlit street. He heard the metallic click of gun-hammers being thumbed back.

'Like I said,' Cranshaw persisted, 'let him free an' we'll go along home.'

'Can't let him out,' Gregg called back. 'Aaron's got the key to the cell, and he's away.'

A burble of cursing came from the cowpunchers, then Cranshaw called, 'Well, that bein' so, we'll have to shoot the lock off the cell door. Come on, boys.'

They were stepping forward, when

Gregg drew his pistol. But the man alongside Cranshaw, Brad Higgins, unleashed a shot from his own gun. The lead grazed Gregg's knuckles, causing him to drop his weapon, having blood welling out from his injured hand. It was a good shot of Higgins, seeing that he was drunk. The sight of Gregg without his pistol brought whoops of glee from all the cowpunchers, and suddenly they were all blazing away, splintering the boardwalk around Gregg's feet, having him dancing a humiliating can-can.

The four cowpunchers were surging forward, as a heavy caliber bullet thundered over their heads, causing them to stop in their tracks, eyes raised towards the flat roof of the marshal's office. Still in his longjohns, Aaron crouched behind the low balustrade, thumbing more ammunition into his Springfield. He was mighty proud how he'd quit Lucy May's bed at the first sound of trouble, and shinned his way up the drainpipe at the back of his office.

He blazed off another shot, anxious not to hit anybody but sending lead close enough to scare the living daylights out of them. All four cow-punchers made a hasty retreat, taking cover on the opposite boardwalk. From here, they directed pistol fire at the marshal's office, the spark of their shots piercing the shadows. Bullets chipped the brickwork close to where Aaron was crouched, and he realized that they did not share his hankering to avoid killing if possible. Meanwhile, Gregg had scampered back inside, nursing his injured hand.

An exchange of shots continued for maybe two minutes, then movement showed in the street and the gunfire died away. Astonishingly, a solidly-built woman wearing a shawl over her nightgown had appeared, stepping off the boardwalk to plant herself firmly in full view of everybody. She was Jenny Holdsworth, wife of the town's black-smith.

'What in all hell's goin' on?' she demanded in a voice loud enough to disturb the whole town. 'Firin' off guns at this time of night is plain disgraceful, wakin' old folks and little'uns. Grown men should know better!'

'We come to get Billy.' Cranshaw's voice explained from the shadows.

'You can't have Billy,' the woman countered. 'He's in jail awaitin' trial for the crime he committed.'

Two more women, wrapped in shawls, had joined Jenny Holdsworth, adding their own tongue-medicine in shrill voices. 'Now you get along home, back to your beds,' one of them cried, 'and leave good, God-fearin' folk in peace. That's if you don't want to land in real trouble!'

Aaron hugged himself against the flat roof, feeling as guilty as a preacher caught with his hand in the church-box. His Springfield had caused more disturbance than all the other artillery put together.

Across the street, he heard the

cowpunchers grumbling amongst themselves, and then, of all things, Seth Cranshaw called out, 'Sorry, Ma'am. We meant no harm.'

One of his companions added support. 'Yes, Ma'am, beggin' your pardon.'

And after that they somehow melted away into the darkness, their horses, hitched to the saloon rail, melting with them. The women returned to their beds, still muttering about the disgrace of such goings on in a civilized community.

Shortly, Aaron gingerly lowered himself down the drainpipe, finding the descent harder on his bones than the climb up. He was glad for the water butt at the bottom to give him respite before his bare feet finally touched ground. He found Gregg in the office, cradling his bloody hand and told him he'd better go across and awake Doctor Clapp for treatment. Come to think of it, the doctor was probably awake already, cursing the disturbance, same as the women.

Gregg told him he'd best get some clothes on instead of running around in his longjohns, otherwise he'd get arrested for indecency.

# 22

It seemed little thought was given to the welfare of Alberto Cordoza by his erstwhile subordinates. He was obviously as popular as a wet dog at a parlor social. The show would no doubt cope quite adequately without his devious and bullying presence. Next day, the great tent came down, the circus packed its bags and the following morning trundled onward, leaving behind in Gilbey's Meadow a horde of litter and associated waste matter for the prairie elements to spirit away.

If Aaron figured that the controversy over the pig would evaporate, dwarfed by more important events, he was mistaken. On the morning that the circus chose to move on, the members of the Town Women's Guild & Temperance Society were again marching along Main Street, new placards held erect.

*Porky for Slaughter. Porky a Disgrace. Death to the Pig.* Some ladies carried horse-whips. Amid strident voices, Emily Grapewrath led her pack like a rampant female bull. But this time, it appeared that word of their intention had been leaked, for a party of some twenty Porky supporters, led by Bent Nose Beecher, formed up, freshly fortified and angry from a rallying meeting at the saloon bar. They advanced towards the women protestors in direct confrontation.

Aaron's nightmare was about to be realized: *civil war between the sexes.*

All minor obstructions, such as a three-legged dog, an old rooster and some youngsters playing hop-scotch, fled the street as the two mobs drew closer. Horses hitched to a rail reared in panic, rolling their eyes and pulling at their tethering reins.

And now the shouting of abuse, the chanting, the cursing was rising to bedlam, turning the air blue, coming from both sides.

Aaron frowned, fear emphasizing the squint lines around his eyes. He wished Gregg was here to help him, but the deputy was still nursing his injured knuckles and had taken Marie-Belle for a picnic, claiming that courting was the best relief for pain ever invented.

The marshal reckoned that his only chance of avoiding mob rule was to place himself between the conflicting parties and proclaim peace in the name of the law, an action that could be likened to suicide. But he had never been one to duck an issue, not often anyway. Accordingly, he now drew a deep breath and stepped into the street with his arms raised, palms held outward in an appeal for peace.

He might just as well have tried to staunch the Red Sea as it flooded back after the parting of the waves.

Incensed females and liquor-fired males slammed together in ferocious battle, all constraint, all chivalry, discarded. Placards were banged against heads, boots slammed into limbs, punches rained, nails scratched, teeth latched onto exposed flesh, horse-whips rose and fell. Emily Grapewrath, her dress in tatters, used her placard as a battering ram, resembling Joan of Arc as she routed the English armies. The formidable Grace Clapp who had never displayed virtues associated with her given name, now was a spitting image of Queen Boudicea, with her bodice ripped away to expose half her bosom. She was using her fists like a prize fighter, standing square, catching Bent Nose Beecher a cruel blow which somehow straightened his snout, bringing tears to his eyes.

But the conflict was far from one-sided, the Porky supporters, sensing an assault on the entire male species, gave no ground, some ladies being dragged to the side and placed across husbands' knees, skirts pulled up to facilitate profound spankings. Straw boaters rolled in the street like tumbleweed and were trampled underfoot. The years of frustration suffered by the down-trodden of both sexes were at last boiling over. Hilda would've loved it, and battered Aaron into pulp.

But the fact was that Aaron was already pulp. At least he felt that way. Caught between the two sides like a nut in a cracker, he'd gone down amid stampeding feet. Now he lay beneath the fallen blacksmith — crushed, trampled, toothless, gasping for breath, flat as a wet leaf — his past sins stampeding through his brain as if he were drowning.

Suddenly, between a woman's wide-spread legs, he glimpsed not only daylight, but a section of boardwalk, and a craving for survival grabbed him. Cranking his bones into motion, he eased himself from beneath the black-smith's bulk, hoisted himself onto his hands and knees and commenced a journey that seemed as long as the Chisholm Trail and twice as dangerous. Somehow he wriggled clear of tangled, struggling bodies and raised what was left of his scrawny frame onto the boardwalk, collapsing in battered exhaustion.

It was then that owl-faced Mayor Tresswell, standing further along, imposed his stentorian voice on the proceedings, sounding like God from Heaven.

*'Hold everythin'. The marshal's hurt!'*

Whether it was compassion for the lawman or battle fatigue that brought a halt to hostilities was debatable. But there descended a gradual quietness, broken only by the moaning of the injured, the panting of weary combatants, and the murmuring of whispers as the mayor's words were passed from mouth to mouth.

And into this sudden peacefulness, a female voice said, 'Oh, poor Aaron, he ain't bad hurt, is he?'

Concern spread across the battlefield like soft rain.

All at once, Aaron found himself being propped up, fussed over, fanned by ladies many of whom were in a state of ragged, bruised semi-nakedness, all backed by sympathetic male voices. One lady in particular, Peewee Poindexter who looked strangely unscathed and cool compared with her fellow Guild members, showed extreme tenderness for Aaron, tears glistening in her eyes. He reckoned that she couldn't have thrown herself into the battle with overmuch enthusiasm.

Despite his marred state, he felt as proud as a man with new underwear. He had never before realized it, but he was a treasured, even loved, institution in Nelly's Nipple.

There was no hospital in town. The most suitable place for treating the injured was at *Porky's Pride*. That afternoon, Doctor Clapp set up his surgery in the bar-room, the lady patients averting their eyes from the shameless painting of Nelly baring her all. The doctor bandaged cut limbs, dolled out liniment for bruising, soothed hurt feelings and generally did good business. He checked Aaron over and assured him he was fit for duty.

Meanwhile, Porky maintained a low profile, resting in his pen.

★   ★   ★

The following Wednesday, the morning stage disgorged Circuit-Judge Isaac C. Marrow. He was seventy years of age, only five foot tall, with a nose resembling a parrot's beak. His eyes glinted like crystallized salt from beneath caterpillar eyebrows. But he was not someone to be dismissed lightly, for, so far, he had sent some twenty-nine men to the rope, having been ordered by the State Governor to inflict the most severe retribution on all wrongdoers. Rumor had it that he had even sentenced a man to the gallows for excessive profanity. Marrow had formed some sort of partnership with the official State Executioner.

On arrival, the judge took up temporary residence at *The Nelly's Nipple Grand Hotel*, which was a somewhat rundown joint, overrun with bed bugs and a special line in monster-cockroaches, but it was the classiest on offer. He had had no time to ponder on the cases he was to adjudicate, but had little doubt that guilty verdicts would ensue and bring the normal maximum sentences. He was somewhat puzzled that he'd been asked to pronounce over matters involving a pig, but would cross that bridge when he came to it.

The trials were to be held in the many-purpose *Porky's Pride* where the normal seating facilities, in readiness for the expected numbers, would be supplemented with pews from the Methodist church. The bar would not be opened until the sentences had been announced. Apparently, the rancher Lyle Cameron had broadcast that he would be present at his son's trial, bringing a crowd of his cowpunchers with him. Cameron had hired a defense lawyer who had already spent an hour with Billy, but appeared to hold out little hope. He'd also agreed to defend

Alberto Cardoza, but drew the line at the pig. Judge Marrow looked forward to a full attendance because he enjoyed playing to the gallery, along with the drama that generally occurred.

He was not to be disappointed.

# 23

The Criminal Sessions Court was called to order. Nelly's Nipple and the surrounding population had turned out in force, even the hurdy-gurdy girls and soiled doves swelling the attendance. Lyle Cameron and his cowpunchers had come sally-hootin' into town like stampeding buffalo. Now the rancher sat at the back, his wooden leg resting on a second chair, a Springfield rifle across his lap, his crazy-wild eyes simmering as if on the brink of outright insanity. Around him crowded a good dozen of his men, all armed. Their spurs jingling, some hunkered down untidily on the floor, so that people had to squeeze around them in passing.

Townsfolk perched two to a seat, and others found comfort on the piano and billiard table. From outside, children and even a dog peered in, noses pressed to the windows.

The legal representation, the judge and lawyers, had their chairs on top of the great bar so they were in full view. Even so, Judge Marrow could scarcely peep over the table before him, due to his dwarf-like stature, and the newly named Straight Nose Beecher passed up a cushion to give him extra height and a downward view of the important papers in front of him. The judge insisted that he had a jar of pickled onions at hand as he had a craving for them. He little realized that the unwashed jar had recently housed an angry rattlesnake, and this may have added something to the flavor of the onions. The reptile was now coiled, only a few feet away, hidden amid the beer kegs, its natural inquisitiveness causing its head to lift.

Gregg Mason had conducted the prisoners to the court, Billy having to be supported as his broken shin hadn't yet knitted, his legs also remaining splinted together to deter him from thoughts of high-tailing from justice. Cardoza was wearing a suit of clothes loaned by the Reverend Grapewrath who was a similar egg-shape to the circus owner, though somewhat smaller. A pigeon egg as opposed to a goose egg, as it were. The sight of Cardoza wearing the reverend's skimpy-fitting suit brought titters to some of the saloon girls.

Across the street, Aaron slumped in his office having always found court sessions tiresome. Especially if you were sharing a seat with somebody like Grace Clapp. Anyway, his own chair was far more comfortable for sore bones. He would snooze until he was called to give evidence.

Just before noon, young Johnny Santo, acting court clerk, came across to request Aaron's presence, and he hobbled after the boy across the street. On the way, he noticed something on the ground. It was his teeth, lying where they popped out during the fracas. He'd forgotten about them. He picked them up, pushed them into his mouth but immediately felt there was something wrong. They'd broken into two bits. He removed them, guessing they'd been trodden on, probably by Emily Grapewrath or Grace Clapp or some other heavy-weight. Still, he might be able to fix them with string. Stuffing them in his pocket, he entered the crowded saloon. The place was thick with baccy smoke and the smell of hot air, most of which had come from the wind-bag judge, the onions having given him gas. Alberto Cardoza was sitting head down, manacled to Gregg, his trial having been concluded.

'Guilty of pig-theft. Clear cut case,' a man whispered in Aaron's ear.

But now the case against Billy Cameron was proceeding, and on being charged with murder he pleaded in a scarcely heard voice, 'Not guilty, your highness.'

'Would you speak up,' the judge said.

'Not guilty, your highness.'

Marrow seemed to appreciate the

elevated form of address. That was probably why he wanted it repeated. Maybe Billy reckoned flattery might save him.

Aaron was the first witness to give evidence and he was sworn in without delay. In his slow drawl, he answered the questions put to him and related his version of events.

'So you actually saw this young man shoot Silas Fogwell?' Marrow enquired, slanting his head for better hearing.

Aaron nodded, 'Yup, your honor,' and the judge appeared to lose interest, figuring the case, like Cardoza's, was open and shut.

When Aaron stood down, he returned to his office, having not fancied the close proximity of Lyle Cameron and his thugs, all of who were looking meaner than centipedes with chilblains.

A big blue-bottle attempted to perch on Aaron's nose. He waved it away, but in so doing his eyes fell on Silas Fogwell's spectacles which had remained on the shelf next to his desk, forgotten about and gathering dust. Aaron picked them up, recalling how Beecher had handed them to him at the time of the undertaker's death. Now, for no known reason, he put them on, hooking the wires behind his ears. They were blue tainted, opaque in appearance, and it took a moment for his eyes to adjust.

Presently, he took them off, slipped them into his vest pocket.

*Could be some sort of evidence,* Beecher had told him.

In the saloon, the third case that day centered around the demeanor of Porky the pig, and the animal was brought into court and encouraged to sit before the judge. Marrow declared that this was the most difficult case of them all, but he said he had often read the Holy Bible and therein Adam and Eve had stitched fig leaves together to make themselves aprons, and that even Christ, when He was naked, was given clothes to wear. It was therefore clear, that the Good Book did not favor any form of nudity and that, in view of Porky having been awarded nigh human privileges, the ladies of Nelly's Nipple had every right to demand a modicum of modesty.

Marrow pronounced all this beneath the painting of naked Nelly who, at that moment, might have been excused for sticking her tongue out.

However, Straight Nose Beecher frowned as he realized that the odds were turning against him. Even Porky's smile seemed a little restrained, his brain striving to absorb the finer technicalities. Beecher slipped him a carrot to lift his spirits.

As the judge's summing up rambled on, the heat in the room became almost intolerable, and the Cameron cow-punchers showed restlessness and made crude noises and showed little respect for the solemnity of the proceedings. At last the jury was invited to remove themselves to a side room to consider their verdict. They were out only five minutes, and when they shuffled back, Seamus Fitzsimmons, the jury foreman, passed the findings to the judge on a scrap of paper.

Aaron had now returned, distancing himself as far as possible from Lyle Cameron and his cronies.

While he scanned the note, Judge Marrow popped another onion into his mouth, making his cheek seem as if it had a carbuncle. Meanwhile, the courtroom lapsed into silence, waiting for the onion to be swallowed. When this happened, the judge debated whether or not to take another, decided against it.

He then announced that all three defendants had been found guilty on all charges, and there was a marked agitation among the cowpuncher fraternity, Lyle Cameron's knuckles showing white as he gripped his Springfield. Aaron knew that the whole situation was poised on a knife edge, could erupt into violence at any moment, but Judge Marrow seemed unaware of the tenseness, being too tied up with his own pompousness.

In a voice full of doom, he asked the defendants to stand, which Cardoza did, but Billy with his broken leg was excused. Porky suddenly seemed to be taking an extreme interest in his rear end. Marrow ignored the misbehavior and turned his attention towards the egg-shaped circus owner.

'You have been found guilty of the charge,' the judge commenced slowly, consulting his notes. 'It is normally a painful duty for a judge to pronounce sentence. But your crime is so heinous that I shed no tears in your case. You have violated the sanctity of this community with a bizarre crime. You mocked the law and caused great concern to many people. You therefore deserve no mercy whatsoever, and I have no hesitation in imposing the maximum sentence.' His next words brought a stunned gasp from those assembled. 'You are to be taken from this court, kept safely and securely in the town's jail until the day appointed for your execution. You are then to be hanged by the neck until you are dead. May God have mercy on your soul.'

Cardoza staggered, his eyes glazed with disbelief, his lip hanging like a blacksmith's apron, but Gregg steadied him. The room was in an uproar. It was like dropping a tomcat into a barrel-full of bulldogs. Somebody yelled out, 'You mean the rope for stealin' a damn pig?'

'Why, that's downright harsh,' Aaron said.

There was now some confusion at the top table. Even Marrow looked puzzled, shuffling his papers and listening to the whisperings of the lawyers.

He stood up on his short legs, hammering with his gavel, shouting, 'Order in court, or I'll adjourn the proceedings!'

Then, in a more condescending voice, he said, 'I do believe the papers have been mixed up. What I should've been advised to say, was that Alberto

Cardoza is sentenced to one year in the State Penitentiary for pig stealing.'

Cordoza, who had been sweating like a . . . pig, now collapsed onto his chair, mopping his brow with relief.

Marrow turned his attention to the trembling Billy Cameron whose guts seemed to have turned to fiddle strings.

'I won't repeat myself,' the judge said. 'Folks might find that boring. All I said previously applies to you. You have sinned and must pay the full penalty. Now the question of the pig . . . '

There occurred an eruption at the back of the court. Lyle Cameron had come to his foot, his chair crashing over. He looked mad enough to eat the devil with his horns on. His surly men, too, were standing up, yelling abuse at the judge. Some had drawn their guns and many of the women present were screaming. Marrow looked aghast at the disrespect being shown to the legal proceedings, hammering in vain with his gavel in an attempt to restore order. Aaron now had visions of the judge being hanged rather than Billy Cameron, and the whole town lapsing into mob rule of lynching, robbery and general bawdiness. Lyle Cameron had always sworn that he was the law, and he didn't need any pussy-footed peace officers to muddy the water.

# 24

As ever, Aaron saw his duty as law-maintainer, and with unusual loudness, he raised his voice into the bedlam, calling for everybody to show respect. Gregg followed suit, and gradually the disorder lessened, though there were still plenty of guns out of their leather.

Aaron felt that he was clutching at straws, but it was all he could think of. He reached into his vest pocket and took out Silas Fogwell's spectacles.

'Hold quiet for a moment,' he called, quelling the last disruption, but he was under no doubt that the calm would only be temporary. The Cameron mob were champing at the bit, waiting for Lyle's nod to enforce their own idea of justice. Billy cringed in his chair, eyes darting about like a frightened rat's.

Aaron held up the spectacles. 'These

belonged to the undertaker,' he stated. 'He was wearin' them at the time he was killed.'

He limped up the court-center aisle and passed the evidence up to the judge. The latter's hand was visibly shaking. The threat of violence had shocked him to the core.

'I think them blue-tinted spectacles were worn by Fogwell for cheatin' purposes,' Aaron said. 'You can see special markin's on the backs of cards with 'em.'

'Are yes,' Judge Marrow said, examining the spectacles closely, anxious to save his skin that he now considered under extreme threat. 'Marks made with phosphorescent ink.'

Support came from an unexpected source. Fogwell's erstwhile apprentice, a young inexperienced man who was now chief and only undertaker in Nelly's Nipple, spoke up.

'Your honor, I think maybe I should mention that when I laid out Mr. Fogwell's body and prepared it for burial, I found this contraption sewn to the inside of his coat. It had a cord attached that ran down to his shoe.' He held up a small metal plate with a playing card fixed to it.

'Why sure, young man,' Judge Marrow said. 'It's what's called a breastplate holdout. You can see where a cord was attached. Using that, a gambler can produce a duplicate pack o' cards by bending his leg.'

A murmur of surprise swept round the room. From the back Lyle Cameron spoke for the first time, his words cutting across other tittle-tattle.

'It's downright clear that Fogwell was a dirty cheat, manipulatin' poor Billy out of his money.'

His cowboys were suddenly shouting agreement, bringing more hammering from Marrow's gavel. The judge seemed to be regaining some of his arrogance.

'The evidence clearly indicates that cheating was taking place,' he announced. 'Not by Billy, but by the undertaker himself. However that is no excuse for shooting a man dead.' He cleared his throat and in a lower voice added, 'But, given the new evidence, I will commute the previous sentence.' He paused, sensing that the atmosphere had become less menacing.

'One year hard labor less remission in the State Pen!' he announced and hammered down his gavel with a finality more often seen when a bargain is sold at an auction.

One of the cowpunchers at the back said, 'Well that's a damn sight fairer. Seems the crime just about deserves that sort of punishment.'

Even Lyle Cameron seemed grudgingly satisfied, for he nodded his bald head in compliance, rammed on his hat and left the courtroom, shoving folks aside as he went. Maybe hard labor might cure the boy's laziness. Holstering their weapons, Lyle's cowpunchers trailed after him, causing a jangling of spurs and scuffing of boots.

After the clattering of departing hoofs faded from outside, a relieved hush settled over the room. Ladies fluttered their handkerchiefs to cool their faces. Then Porky snorted, anxious no doubt, after such a long session, to return to the convenience in his pen. Attention turned towards him.

'And how about the pig?' somebody asked.

Judge Marrow was glad to reassume his authority.

'To be slaughtered,' he said.

Unseen by others, a large tear trickled down Peewee Poindexter's cheek. It was not induced by the closeness of Marrow's jar of onions but by the harshness of sentence.

The judge popped a final onion into his mouth, gathered up his papers and left the court. Having collected his baggage from the hotel, he boarded the next stage out of town.

Emily Grapewrath was determined that the law should be fully applied, and this time she prevailed upon the town butcher to act as official executioner. He set aside time on the following

Saturday afternoon to cut the beast's throat.

Straight Nose Beecher, on Porky's behalf, made a special plea — that the condemned animal be given freedom to wander the streets where he chose during the last days of his life. Under persuasion from Peewee Poindexter, the minister's wife reluctantly agreed.

Apart from the ladies of the Guild, few considered there was cause for celebration in the town, but as Beecher pointed out, two criminals had got their just desserts and it would seem that law and order had returned to Nelly's Nipple, although the judiciary rulings had not all been to his liking. As much to lift his own spirits as those of others, Beecher called a grand party in the saloon with drinks on the house. It gave everybody an opportunity to shake Porky's trotter and bid him a formal farewell. Invites were sent to all and sundry, though no big bug ladies accepted. None the less, on Friday evening, the saloon was crowded and refreshments were laid on and served by Lucy May and her soiled doves, whilst Violette La Plante exercised her tonsils to the accompaniment of the piano.

Aaron was enjoying the freebies, stocking up for lost time, not giving a damn that cream was smeared across his cookie-duster.

Standing near the billiard table, he noticed how Porky had trotted over to him.

The pig could be tiresome at times, begging the way he did, his snout wrinkling as he picked up scent of a man's sandwich, squatting on his haunches, his cloven hoofs pawing the air. It seemed that he had at last forgiven Aaron for applying his boot so firmly, but the marshal didn't feel inclined to feed the beast, deciding that he best build up his own strength for the future, whereas Porky did not have that need.

'Sandwich is real tasty,' he commented to Straight Nose Beecher who had sauntered over.

Beecher nodded. 'Sam Brewer, my head barkeep, caught a rattlesnake behind some beer kegs yesterday. Had them sandwiches 'specially made up.'

Aaron's hand paused half way to his mouth. 'You mean . . . ?'

'Sure.'

Aaron peeled back the top layer of his sandwich, saw the reptile's head reclining comfortably on its pillow of buttered bread, its eye upturned. To his dying day, Aaron swore that the eye winked at him. He lowered the top layer and munched on, telling himself that one sort of meat was as good as another.

He slept comfortably that night, cozy as a toad under a cabbage leaf, enjoying the pleasure of cell comfort, the previous inmates having been shipped off to less salubrious accommodation.

But Aaron would not have slumbered so well had he known what fate had lined up.

Even Porky would have cause to remember the following day, and it wasn't only because it was ear-marked for him to receive his angel-wings, piggy version.

# 25

Thanks to Doctor Clapp's pills, Will Brosker recovered from his heart trouble, though he would never forget the shock of when he'd turned to find a great lion breathing down his collar. Godamighty, that had been real trauma! Doc Clapp had told him that if he soaked up any more hard liquor, he'd be as good as dead. He had spent three days resting at Nelly's Nipple, heeding the advice to stay away from the saloon. He turned his mind to other old habits: bank robbery for one.

As he collected his pills from the saw-bones's drugstore, his eyes fell on Poindexter's Western Bank directly opposite, seeing the town's wealthy residents trotting in and out. He reckoned that the bank had more money than it knew what to do with. He had no inclination to return to

Cameron's ranch. He was sick of being treated like a dog by the old man. What he needed was some easy pickings before he quit this territory, and the bank seemed to offer the ideal opportunity. He eventually fell out with the doctor, the latter having tried to charge him a staggering sum for the treatment. Brosker had refused to pay, stomped out, collected his bay horse from the livery and taken to the hills south of town. From here, camping cold, he prepared his plan.

Saturday morning dawned with the sun rapidly rising to its seething fury. It would not be a good day, town Butcher Ed Rainslip concluded. He was not in the habit of slaughtering the meat he retailed nowadays, but he was familiar with the methods.

He had enjoyed Porky's company at the saloon as much as most other men, and he did not view the task ahead with any relish. However, never one to ignore a quick profit, he had struck a bargain with Beecher and accordingly had placed a notice outside his butcher's window extolling the deliciousness of fresh pork chops and joints that could be enjoyed immediately or salted away for winter use, indicating that a supply would be available that very evening, and the first five customers would get a free trotter.

Mathematics had never been Rainslip's strong point.

He put the final touches to his knife sharpening, honing it on an oil-stone. He then took out his sticker and boner, reminding himself that by shortly after three o'clock that afternoon, the deed would be done.

★   ★   ★

Banks in the West were still scarce in number, and folks tended to carry their worldly wealth, hard-time tokens and stamp currencies around with them or hide them under their beds, all of which was risky — and tokens and stamps soon got soiled. So when James

Poindexter founded Poindexter's Western Bank in Nelly's Nipple, the locals were happier than lost souls finding heaven. Maybe it was a sodbuster bank, but it never issued wild-cat money. It somehow signified the town's coming of age, and there was a mad stampede to deposit all available cash in its vault. Of course this was fine unless the bank burned down — or it was robbed.

As Will Brosker edged his bay horse along the street that Saturday morning, everywhere was quiet and nobody gave him a second glance. He drew level with the bank just as James Poindexter was raising his blinds and opening shop.

Poindexter was president of the bank, as well as being manager, teller, cashier bookkeeper and general dog's body. He added sophistication by wearing a boiled shirt, string tie, black coat and pin-stripe trousers and hoped shortly to employ an assistant.

Thankful that no other customers had yet arrived, Brosker dismounted, hitched the bay lightly to the outside rail. He grabbed the big grain sack from his saddle bag, pulled his red bandanna over his face, drew his pistol and made his entry.

Poindexter, half spectacles riding his nose, busy behind the wooden counter loading his coin box with silver dollars, scarcely looked up. Not noticing his customer's aggressive stance, he said, 'Morning, Mr. Brosker, what can we do for you this fine morning?'

Brosker stopped the other side of the cashier's grill. 'I ain't Brosker,' he lied.

Now Poindexter raised his glance. 'Well, if you're not Will Brosker, you're wearing the exact-same bandanna as him. Bright red with spots of dirt on it. Dust must be pretty bad today for you to hoist it over your face.'

'The bandanna's different from Brosker's,' the renegade cowpuncher argued, not liking to be crossed. 'This is no joke.' He raised his gun. 'I want all the money you've got. And that includes everythin' in the vault. Now unlock the counter so's I can come through and give you a hand!'

Poindexter all at once appreciated the gravity of the situation.

'But that's robbery,' he gasped. His face as pale as skimmed milk.

'And robbery . . . *it's unlawful!*'

Brosker thumbed back the hammer of his pistol with a loud click. 'Don't bullshit me. I told you, unlock the counter.'

Poindexter glanced around seeking support, but there was none. He looked back at Brosker, saw how his split-lip was twitching, how his eyes were burning like coals. He started to shake, moved along the counter and slid back the security bolt. As he turned towards the back-room vault, Brosker's gun jabbed against his spine like a cowpuncher's prod-pole.

Using the combination, Poindexter had only just opened the walk-in vault, and Brosker gasped appreciatively at the sight of shelf-upon-shelf of neatly bundled paper-money, mostly greenbacks, together with bonds and sheets of revenue stamps. He almost dropped his gun as he feverishly began scooping everything into the grain sack that the grim-faced Poindexter held for him. It was as he cleared the last shelf that the bell on the counter rang.

'Mr. Poindexter,' Mrs. Rainslip called, unaware of vault room events. 'I've come to draw some money, if you please.'

'Tell her you're sold out,' Brosker hissed through his split lip.

Poindexter swallowed hard. His voice came with a noticeable quiver. 'No cash available right now, Mrs. Rainslip. Can you call by later?'

The lady muttered dissatisfaction, but left the bank. Having recently been accused of murdering her son's rat, she was no slouch when it came to smelling another one. Outside, she gathered up her skirts and hurried to the marshal's office.

Hoisting the bulging sack across his shoulder, Brosker pushed Poindexter towards the till. 'All the coin as well,' he snapped. He felt downright hot behind his mask and he ordered the bank man to make haste, but not to leave a cent.

Poindexter complied, shaking with fury. He scooped the coin into three separate bags, it being too weighty for one. As Brosker attempted to gather them up, he cursed. 'Too damn heavy. Change it into notes.'

'You'll have to do it yourself,' Poindexter advised. 'You got them all.'

Brosker opened up a bag of coin, was about to start counting when his simple mind registered the stupidity of it. Cursing again, he gathered up two bags of coin.

'You stay here until I'm clear of town, otherwise I'll . . . come back and shoot you dead!'

He holstered his gun, staggered from the bank under the weight of coin and the huge sack of notes.

The bay horse was edgy as he was unhitched and the man hoisted himself into the saddle. The animal had been real nervous since being followed by that circus lion. Now he sagged slightly under the extra load as Brosker jabbed his heels into him. Even so they went forward at a fair clip.

This was hastened even more, as Aaron McLean, still in his longjohns and closely followed by Mrs. Rainslip, rushed from his office and blasted off with his Springfield. The lead skinned the bay's hip, causing him to rear but he came down galloping, pounding on at even greater speed, Brosker somehow clinging to both his saddle and his ill-gotten gains. Meanwhile, more folks were appearing from doorways, shouting with alarm. But Brosker grimaced with satisfaction, sensing that he would be out of town soon, leaving them all behind.

It was just before he drew level with the saloon, that Porky, enjoying freedom of the town on his last morning, trotted rapidly into the street, his trotters a blur of mincing steps. He stopped directly in the path of the galloping horse, ears pricked, snout raised towards the pound of approaching hoofs. He reared up as if in anger, his own hoofs pawing the air. When these resumed contact with the ground, he stood forelegs planted well apart, stubbornly indicating his intention to make a stand.

The bay, no doubt wondering if this sudden apparition was lion clad in pig's clothing, whinnied in terror and skidded to a halt with such abruptness, that Brosker, handicapped by his burden, lost his grip on the saddle and shot forward past the horse's neck. He hit the ground shoulder-first with crunching force, his sacks of loot bursting open to spew coin and dollar-bills across the street, the slight morning breeze plucking the latter up into a cloud like a pauper's dream.

The bay continued its dash from town, circling the pig by the widest possible margin. Meanwhile Brosker lay groaning. Aaron came rushing up, leveling his rifle at the fallen man but soon realizing that weaponry would not be needed. Meanwhile, a crowd of angry townsfolk followed up and crowded around Brosker, while others were already gathering the scattered loot.

'For God's sake don't just stand there,' Brosker gasped at Aaron. 'I'm bad hurt. Get Doctor Clapp.'

# 26

The morning had passed in a whirl of frantic activity and Aaron's jail was again blessed with an inmate, though it was anticipated that Brosker would be sent to the state capital for trial, rather than having to go through the rigmarole with Judge Marrow again.

In next to no time, the dreaded hour of three showed on the town clock, and there gathered around the pig-pen a small select band of citizens who would witness the enactment of the law, mainly members of the town council. These included Mayor Tresswell, Straight Nose Beecher, Aaron McLean, James Poindexter the President of the Bank, still flushed from his morning's fright, and three other stern-faced men. Lucy May had come along to support Aaron, him feeling somewhat sick and thinking he maybe had a touch of rattlesnake fever brought on by overeating. Final member of the group was, of course, Ed Rainslip the butcher, suitably garbed in his striped apron and armed with his knife.

There was no sign of the pig. He was sleeping unsuspectingly in his shelter.

Standing by the pen gate, Rainslip gave Beecher a meaningful nod. With ceremonial gravity, the saloon keeper inserted his fingers between his lips, paused, and then unleashed the piercing whistle. *Last time*, he thought, and his was not the only eye that showed the glisten of a tear.

There now sounded the familiar snort from within the shelter, the familiar sound of heavy weight being lifted, and shortly Porky showed himself, his small eyes blinking away his sleepiness, his expression signaling the usual:

'Yeah, watcha want?'

Lucy May had begun to sob mournfully and Aaron slipped his arm around her, comforting her as best he could as

216

the ordeal unfolded. Rainslip slid back the bolt with a grating sound and he swung the gate open. He took a deep breath and stepped into the pen, binding rope in one hand, knife in the other.

'Porky,' he murmured huskily, 'come here, my old friend.'

★   ★   ★

An hour earlier, with Emily Grapewrath and Grace Clapp having gone to Fallow Springs for the day intending to buy mulberry shrubs, Peewee Poindexter had convened an urgent meeting of the Guild. In general, they were a sorry sight, still displaying bruises and cuts, and Esther Brown had her arm in a sling.

Three ladies were late in arriving and, to Peewee's distress, it was two-thirty before proceedings opened.

Peewee had never appeared so authoritative. In an incisive and urgent voice, she drew attention to the events of the morning, to the way that the town would have been completely undermined, her husband ruined and individuals bankrupted if Brosker had escaped with his ill-gotten gains. Nelly's Nipple would have been brought to its knees, so impoverished that it would have faded into history. But the community owed its salvation to the courage, the single handed dedication of one individual, who had been prepared to lay down his life for others.'

'Yes, Aaron did a good job,' a lady commented.

Peewee bristled slightly. 'Yes, he did, but it was Porky who enabled him to capture Brosker. Had it not been for that pig's valor, I tremble to think what a state we'd be in now.'

Her words brought a surprised whispering to the assembly.

'We agree that the pig got in Brosker's way, made him fall off his horse,' Mrs. Brown said, 'but that was probably an accident.'

'No,' Peewee blazed. 'He stood firm,

could have been shot dead, but he stood there, solid as a rock, using his body to bar Brosker's escape.'

'Well, that being so, what can we do, award him a medal, posthumously?'

'Or maybe erect a statue?'

'Or even have him stuffed!'

Peewee eyed the wall clock. The minutes were melting away fast. She could see the big hand jerking through the seconds. It was ten minutes before three — no, nine before three!

'Ladies,' she said, 'Judge Marrow is long gone. He'll never know whether or not his sentence is carried out. Porky is due to die in a few minutes, but we can save him. A unanimous plea might . . .'

'Emily and Grace would be furious!'

'Emily and Grace aren't here! They'll be as glad as the rest of us that our life savings are still in the bank. Who knows what they'd say? Just think what Porky has done for us. We've got to make the decision — immediately. It's a matter of life or death!'

* * *

Porky was amused at first, thinking it was some sort of game, as Ed Rainslip circled rope around his stumpy right foreleg and linked it with his left rear leg. But when the rope was drawn tight, knotted, and Porky was obliged to roll onto his back, his sense of humor was waning, the first squeal of complaint rising from his lungs.

Rainslip placed his thumb against the pig's throat, selected the exact spot. It would be a bloody business and he was glad of his large apron.

Around the pen, the observers stood in maudlin silence. Lucy May had averted her eyes, snuggling against Aaron's chest in a manner which stirred protective instincts, even his love, for her.

'Will he scream when the knife goes in?' she whispered in a trembling voice.

'No, he'll die quick,' Aaron soothed, though he wasn't sure.

It was then that a patter of running feet sounded.

Everybody in the group turned to see Peewee Poindexter rushing pell-mell towards them, one hand holding her lead-weighted skirts above her knees, the other keeping her boater in place. She stumbled, but righted herself and ran on.

'Stop! Stop!' she shrieked.

Within the pen, Ed Rainslip straightened up, glad enough to delay the dreaded moment.

Peewee was totally breathless, but she reached them, taking her husband's arm for support.

'The ladies of the Guild,' she somehow panted out. 'They've . . . voted unanimously . . . voted that a plea be made to save Porky. After what he did for the town . . . showing he was a real hero and all, he deserves to be . . . rewarded.'

'You mean they've withdrawn their objection to havin' Porky around?' Beecher asked, amazement spreading across his straight-nosed face.

Peewee bobbed her head and cried out, 'Yes. Judge Marrow need never know.'

There was a long pause, each person chewing over her words.

'It would be breakin' the law,' somebody said. 'Wouldn't be right.'

'No harm in breakin' the law,' Aaron commented, 'if the law never knows.'

'You're the law, Marshal. You'd know.'

'I'll turn a blind eye,' Aaron said.

'The pig did us a good turn,' Mayor Tresswell said. 'He don't deserve to be treated like a criminal.'

There was general agreement by an overwhelming vote of seven to one.

Ed Rainslip had never been more willing to be thwarted. He let out a grunt, then he plunged his knife downward, slicing through the rope, allowing Porky to scramble onto his trotters, snort scoffingly, and reclaim his dignity.

Sometimes he just couldn't fathom humans.

# 27

Of course Emily Grapewrath and Grace Clapp were put out by what had happened, saying the law had been flouted, but they eventually accepted that Porky didn't deserve to be slaughtered. To save face, they demanded that the town's name be changed from Nelly's Nipple, considering it an insult. At a meeting of the town council, it was decided to rename the town in Porky's honor.

With a wry smile, Mayor Tresswell considered that something with a more manly ring about it would be preferable.

So, if you look on a map today, you won't find Nelly's Nipple, but you will see *Porky's Pecker*.

One day soon after, the marshal of Porky's Pecker was spooning beans from a can, his feet up on the desk. A couple of beans dropped to the floor, but he scooped them up and popped them into his mouth. He remembered how things had been on that night the trouble started, when Billy Cameron had shot Silas Fogwell. It seemed like a hundred years ago, yet it was only a few weeks. So much water had flowed under the proverbial bridge since *Porky's Pride* had opened its batwings. Still, he now figured law and order had been restored in town, apart from a couple of minor misdemeanors. Namely the theft of Mrs. Clapp's drawers from her clothes line, and the report he'd received from Dave Rainslip the butcher's son that his mother had murdered Arthur his pet rat. Both cases were subject to further investigation.

Now, he glanced up as Straight Nose Beecher and his heel-sniffing pal Porky popped into the office, bringing some doughnuts, commonly known as bearsign. Beecher dropped into a chair. Porky settled himself on the floor with a grin on his face.

'I never seen a pig grin so much as this one,' Aaron remarked, sucking the plum preserve out of his bear-sign.

Beecher smiled. 'Can hardly blame him. I guess he had the last laugh on them stuck up ladies. You know how they went on 'bout how he saved the prosperity of the town, standing his ground when Brosker was charging down the street, all horns and rattles. How he never batted an eyelid, but blocked the escape.'

Aaron nodded, thumbing sugar from his cookie-duster. 'Sure didn't flinch. Stood his ground like George Armstrong Custer.'

'Thing is, Porky didn't have a clue what was happenin'.'

'How come?' Aaron asked.

'Just to confirm what I suspected, we gave him an eye test yesterday, and you'd never believe it, but he's as blind as a mole in a hole. Can't see a damn thing. That's why he sticks to my heel like glue, so I can give him a steer to get

around. I ain't tellin' them ladies
though.'

'Well I be damned!' Aaron explained,
and both men were overcome with
mirth. Porky kept his grin.

★   ★   ★

That afternoon the Reverend Grapewrath passed by and, in the hope of
saving the marshal's soul, gave him a
Holy Bible. Aaron opened it at random,
skipping past the Ner begat Kish and
Kish begat . . . and so on. In Ephesians
Chapter 4, he read how truth was
always spoken in love. This made him
wonder if all the tongue lashings and
snake-poison scorn Hilda had poured
on him had been her way of expressing
deep-held affection. And reading the
Bible somehow brought Hilda more
and more into his mind, for she had
been a devout churchgoer. In fact he
would have gone with her, tipped his
hat to the Lord, but she always
discouraged him saying that, having

committed so many sins, it would be hypocritical for him to enter the house of God. And anyway, he didn't have any decent Sunday-best to wear, none of his clothes, she said, being fit to dust a fiddle with.

Aaron's rheumatism seemed to be getting worse of late; he felt generally run down. Maybe this was due to the trouble of recent weeks. But the truth was, he was beginning to feel his age and maybe he wouldn't make old bones. The thought came to him that soon he would meet up with Hilda again, that she would be waiting for him, arms reaching out to push him off in case he got too close to her, and, if he dodged, ducking her lips as a second line of defense, to avoid his slobbering.

Yes, they would soon be together again, for he had received a letter from the Governor of the Women's Penitentiary, saying that Hilda McLean had been granted remission for good behavior and would be released at next Christmas time. *Good behavior*, he

227

thought, or was it because they couldn't stand her viper-tongue any more? She would have served just twelve years for her crime of murder. Mind you, Aaron had never figured she was guilty, despite the fact that those Pinkerton Detectives had been trailing her for years, collecting proof that she had butchered her first husband. Of course Aaron hadn't known anything about her past when he'd fallen in love with her. Nothing about it, until ten years of married life had ground by.

He'd never forget the day those detectives had arrested her; her face was so pale. He'd been as mortified as she was. He'd sat through most of the trial, hearing how she'd killed her first husband with a meat-cleaver because he was bone idle and useless. Her claims of innocence had been to no avail. The judge had been severe: fifteen years in jail. But now they were letting her out, three years early.

Hilda had written to him only once during her years of being locked away, and that was to discourage him from visiting her, because she'd apparently met up with some really classy ladies who'd fallen on hard times similar to her own. She'd said not to visit because she'd spread the word that she was a society woman who'd taken a rich businessman as her second husband, and she thought it would be disrespectful to her friends if Aaron showed up.

But through all those years, he'd never ceased to remember her and miss her, and when Christmas came, he guessed they could continue life where they'd left off. He lifted the photograph of her and gazed at it. He smoothed it with his baccy-stained finger, spat on the glass twice and wiped the dust off with his sleeve.

We do hope that you have enjoyed reading this large print book.

Did you know that all of our titles are available for purchase?

We publish a wide range of high quality large print books including:
**Romances, Mysteries, Classics**
**General Fiction**
**Non Fiction and Westerns**

Special interest titles available in large print are:
**The Little Oxford Dictionary**
**Music Book, Song Book**
**Hymn Book, Service Book**

Also available from us courtesy of Oxford University Press:
**Young Readers' Dictionary**
**(large print edition)**
**Young Readers' Thesaurus**
**(large print edition)**

For further information or a free brochure, please contact us at:
**Ulverscroft Large Print Books Ltd.,**
**The Green, Bradgate Road, Anstey,**
**Leicester, LE7 7FU, England.**
**Tel:** (00 44) **0116 236 4325**
**Fax:** (00 44) **0116 234 0205**

When former hired gun Calvin Taylor took the job of sheriff of Oxford County, New Mexico, it was for one reason only — to catch, or kill, the notorious Arizona Kid, and pick up the fifteen hundred dollars reward the governor had secretly offered. Taylor found himself on the trail of the infamous gang known as the Regulators, hunting down a man who'd once been his friend. The pursuit became, in every sense, a journey of death.